A  DALA

By

Sharon Fellows

Copyright © Sharon Fellows 2019
This book is sold subject to the condition that it shall not, by way of trade or otherwise, be lent, resold, hired out, or otherwise circulated without the publisher's prior consent in any form of binding or cover other than that in which it is published and without a similar condition including this condition being imposed on the subsequent publisher.
The moral right of Sharon Fellows has been asserted.
ISBN-13: 9781687794000

DEDICATION

Thank you to my mom Sue, sister Helen, and friend of many years Pat Lane, for their support and encouragement in me writing my first novel.

Without your support, I could not have done it.

CONTENTS

Prologue 1
Chapter 1 *April 2009 – Meeting Richard* 3
Chapter 2 *Sarah* 7
Chapter 3 *London* 10
Chapter 4 *The News* 14
Chapter 5 *Life After Maud* 17
Chapter 6 *The Inquest and Funeral* 20
Chapter 7 *Opportunities* 22
Chapter 8 *Dala* 26
Chapter 9 *The Plan* 36
Chapter 10 *Final Visit* 39
Chapter 11 *Return to UK* 44
Chapter 12 *Final Part of the Plan* 53
Chapter 13 *Sarah – Dependent on Richard* 57
Chapter 14 *Travel to Inveralligin* 59
Chapter 15 *First Night Apart* 61
Chapter 16 *Inveralligin* 65
Chapter 17 *Holiday* 75
Chapter 18 *Preparation* 78
Chapter 19 *Start of the Holiday* 81
Chapter 20 *The Flight* 85
Chapter 21 *Arrival* 87
Chapter 22 *Plan Underway* 89
Chapter 23 *The Realisation* 98
Chapter 24 *On the Run* 101
Chapter 25 *The Swap Is Known* 109
Chapter 26 *Hunt for Richard and Dala* 114
Chapter 27 *Tracy* 120
Chapter 28 *Alone in France* 134

Chapter 29 *Lia and Richard Taylor* 140
Chapter 30 *Life in Inveralligin* 144
Chapter 31 *Lia* 150
Chapter 32 *10 Years Later* 153
ABOUT THE AUTHOR 173

This is a work of fiction. Names, characters, businesses, organizations, places, events and incidents either are the product of the author's imagination or are used fictitiously. Any resemblance to actual persons, living or dead, events, or locales is entirely coincidental.

Prologue

The small group, our close friends Angela and Pete, our long-term guests, and Ross, the man I owe so much to, have been singing Happy Birthday to Lia; she looks like she is going to cry with happiness at the surprise birthday party.

Lia is 30 today and still looks as lovely as the day I first met her just over 11 years ago.

I look around at the happy faces surrounding me and ask myself, was it so wrong, what I did years back?

If I had not done what I had then Lia would not be celebrating her birthday today.

What is it they say, "Let he without sin cast the first stone"?

I am a decent and hard-working person and I would never intentionally hurt anyone. Things had to be done though and people did get hurt.

What I did was for the greater good. Yes, there had been casualties but that could not have been avoided.

Things would be different now of course, with modern technology and facial recognition systems; back then I relied on human error to achieve my ultimate goal.

Angela interrupts my thoughts. "Come on, you, we are waiting to take the photo."

"Sorry, I was miles away." I jump up and put my arm around Lia, smiling at the camera.

Chapter 1

April 2009 – Meeting Richard

"Richard, come and join us." Maud is a big fan of Richard. He had arrived at the local church a month ago and had become an active member of the weekly coffee mornings and local fund-raising events.

Perfect son-in-law material for her granddaughter, Sarah.

Maud would never normally think that anyone was good enough for her granddaughter, however Richard seemed ideal.

A bit on the small side, probably no more than five feet seven inches and quite pasty looking. That aside though, he had a good heart and was showing more than a little interest in Sarah.

As Richard joins them, Sarah blushes. Sarah has had very little to do with the opposite sex. Having attended an all-girls school and choosing not to go on the usual girly nights out she was very naïve of men and of the world in general.

Not one for hobbies and meeting friends, Sarah's life consisted of looking after her grandmother.

After Sarah had left high school, Maud unfortunately had a bad fall whilst out shopping and could not get about easily; even now she still had trouble, with the crippling arthritis making it worse.

Sarah was happy enough. Maud had been her mum and dad rolled into one, after her parents had died in a car crash when she was just two years old. Maud had brought Sarah up on her own, following the death of her daughter.

Maud's husband Ronald had died of heart failure two years before the death of her daughter.

Sarah was kept busy going to church meetings, local fundraising and more recently a book club; she could not grumble.

She had never been one that was interested in parties or a career and was quite content spending time with Maud, the closest person to her.

One thing that Sarah wishes she could do is go abroad. Maud would never contemplate going abroad, openly stating that planes could drop out of the sky and ships could sink, just like the *Titanic*.

Richard has a place in France; he has a property in Nice and has told Sarah this is the second-largest French city on the Mediterranean coast with spectacular views and excellent shopping. He loves the laid-back attitude of the local people and French cuisine.

He has promised Sarah that one day he will take her there so she can see it for herself.

As Maud and Richard discuss the lack of church funding for some repair work, Sarah dreams of what Richard's place is like in the French Riviera sun.

Richard had been back in the UK for two weeks, looking for the right base, and had one day by accident come across the little village of North Cotes near Grimsby.

He had watched Maud and Sarah from afar, attending the flower arrangements on the grave of Maud's late husband.

Sarah had lovely long dark hair and large brown eyes, about the right age, height and weight for the type of girl he was looking for.

Richard had taken the plunge and had started a conversation with Maud and Sarah when they returned to the car park, explaining he was new to the area and keen to get involved with the local community.

Sarah had learned that Richard originally had relatives that lived in Lincolnshire and he was touring this part of the country out of interest during a break from his business in Nice.

Richard had a beachside snack bar near a public beach called Villefranche-sur-Mer. He had been able to purchase the snack bar by using his inheritance from his Grandad who had died five years previously.

His snack bar is not on the beach directly, as he has told Sarah that the beach area is very small and his is placed alongside other bars and restaurants opposite the beach.

He has been able to take a break from the business as a couple of the locals will run the snack bar in his absence. They have worked for him for three years and he considers them entirely trustworthy.

Whilst touring the UK, Richard is having his house decorated and a new kitchen area installed. He did not want to be about when the work was being done and thought that now was the right time to come back to the UK and to go home when the work was complete.

Chapter 2

Sarah

I did not ever think I would be interested in seeing anybody, but Richard has changed all that. He is funny, kind and caring. He has given me the confidence to wear nicer clothes, use make-up and has shown me what fun is.

Until I met Richard, I had never been to a theme park. It was one of the best days of my life; going on a roller coaster at Alton Towers was the most frightening and exciting experience.

As a child I had never had the opportunity as Grandma was too frightened and even back then she could not get about much.

Other children had talked about such days out, but I had never experienced it until now at the age of 21.

Richard is 10 years older than me and this makes

me feel safe and secure. He has many life experiences.

Last week we went to the cinema followed by a lovely meal at a small Italian restaurant. I did not like to tell Richard that I had never eaten Italian food before mainly because I had nobody to try it with and Grandma only eats plain English food.

The wine made me all giggly as I normally only ever have a small glass of sherry.

It was this night that Richard kissed me for the first time.

Back at home, Grandma was asleep, and he pulled me into his arms and kissed me; not just a peck but like I had seen in the movies, passionately, stroking my hair and letting his hands wander down over my body.

I am a virgin and I do not know what to expect. Over the years I have lost touch with school friends and so I have nobody to talk to about this.

Richard is taking me away next weekend to London; I know what will happen and I am very excited but nervous at the same time.

The fact Grandma approves means a lot. I have introduced boys in the past and she made plain her disapproval.

It is all arranged. Grandma will have a neighbour come in a few times a day to check on her and she has promised to keep the phone and asthma inhaler with her at all times.

Chapter 3

London

All packed, Richard is putting the cases in the car.

I am so excited; Richard has said he will take me to Madame Tussauds and on the London Eye.

Just pulling off the drive and Richard pulls in. "Sorry, I have forgotten my mobile, I know I said no work, just for an emergency." He winks and jumps out the car, saying he will be five minutes.

Maud looks up with delight at Richard coming back in. He picks up his mobile, saying he only just remembered it in time.

Richard bends forward to kiss Maud goodbye; he does not have much time.

He suddenly pulls the support pillow from behind her back and thrusts it over her face, pressing as hard as he can. Maud is struggling, Richard is impressed;

give her credit, she is a lot stronger than he thought.

This should be over soon. He speaks soothingly to her, telling her that he is very sorry, but she has to go and it's nothing personal.

Eventually after what seems like 10 minutes she no longer struggles; he holds on for a while longer just to make sure.

It was unfortunate that Maud had to go. She had been asking too many probing questions about his business in Nice; how well it was doing, who was managing it whilst he was away and if she could see photos of his house.

Too many questions and Richard could not risk losing Sarah now, not after all the effort of finding her. It had been hard finding that special someone, his ideal girl.

He had tried to do it as quickly and painlessly as possible. He liked old Maud, but the risk factor was too great.

Never mind, he would be there to pick up the pieces and look after Sarah. He would look after her and make sure she was OK.

Sarah would be wondering where he was. He quickly plumps up the pillow and places behind

Maud's back, carefully picking up her phone and asthma inhaler and placing them on the floor.

Maud's head has now fallen to the side. Richard is pleased as this looks more natural. He wonders how long it will take for Maud to go cold. He knows that this happens; his grandad had been all cold in the funeral parlour when he went to say goodbye.

At last, no more questions from Maud, this would be a weight off his shoulders.

Back in the car he tells Sarah he had difficulty finding his mobile and eventually found it in the kitchen.

As they pull off the drive, Sarah waves at the house thinking that Maud may be able to see her.

The journey to London was quite smooth; some traffic hold-ups on the M25 but not too much of a delay.

The hotel has limited parking and Richard is able to get the last available space.

It was a modern hotel that had several restaurants and offered spa treatments. Sarah was pleased with the lovely room that Richard had booked, a superior double bedroom with a balcony.

Richard had told Sarah she could pick which

restaurant to go to later in the evening.

Sarah is shocked at the amount of people in the streets. Coming from a small village, the crowds seem overwhelming. Richard tells her this is a quiet time and later this afternoon it will be much busier with people leaving work for the day.

Richard suggests they start at Harrods, have a light lunch there and browse the shop, perhaps find a present for Maud then move on to see Buckingham Palace before going on the London Eye. They can go to Madame Tussauds tomorrow morning followed by St Paul's Cathedral.

Chapter 4

The News

Sarah did not hear the news until they returned to the hotel. They had taken their mobiles with them but had not heard the calls due to the noise levels whilst sightseeing.

Sarah was devastated and blamed herself for leaving Maud. The neighbour had found Maud just two hours after they had left.

It was believed Maud had died from a bad asthma attack although the coroner would need to confirm this; an autopsy was to be carried out.

Her inhaler had been found on the floor by the chair. It was thought that Maud had tried to use the inhaler and panicked when she had accidently dropped it, making the attack worse than it would have been.

All that Sarah could think about was that if she

had been there then Maud would have had her inhaler and she would still be alive.

The fact she had been out enjoying herself when Maud died, most likely frightened and in pain, made it even worse.

She knew that the asthma had been bad, but she thought it had been under control.

*

I had taken Sarah to the hospital mortuary late evening for the official identification to confirm that the body was in fact Maud.

Sarah had not wanted to see Maud as she wanted to remember her as she was, not cold in a mortuary. The identification needed to be done, so I had persuaded Sarah to do it that evening rather than wait for the following day, so it would be done with and she would not have to worry about doing this the following day.

I had even gone into the mortuary with Sarah, to support her whilst she confirmed it was Maud and said her goodbyes. Also, for me, it had been a chance to make sure there were no tell-tale signs of a struggle.

*

Sarah did not know how she was going to continue without Maud. Even having Richard with her would not be enough to fill the emptiness she felt. She felt shock, anger and guilt all at the same time and could not stem the tears.

That night back at Maud's house, Richard stayed with Sarah. It was for the best as Sarah was in no fit state to be left on her own.

He had held her hand, listened to her, comforted her throughout the evening, made her cups of tea and gave her the odd glass of brandy for the shock. It was towards midnight that Richard could not hold back anymore.

He knew that he shouldn't have but he did all the same. Seeing her so upset, all he wanted to do was comfort her, one thing led to another and he took her virginity in the lounge where Maud had died.

It was too much. Looking into those big brown eyes, he could not have controlled his male urges any longer, he had needed to do this although he felt such guilt after.

Sarah had cried all night which had not helped.

Chapter 5

Life After Maud

I don't know what I would have done without Richard over the last few weeks. He has been fantastic, a shoulder to cry on, making sure I ate and drank, helping with the funeral preparations and even informing people of Grandmother's death when I could not face doing it.

All my life, it has been just me and my grandma; we were closer than most mothers and daughters as she was both mother and father rolled into one.

I never felt I missed out not having siblings as I know no different. I had a great childhood and participated in many after-school clubs, I had various hobbies ranging from swimming for the county to horse riding, I had even got a couple of trophies for both.

I mixed well with other children and was quite happy, although when it got to the late teenage years,

I was not interested in going out drinking and clubbing and I lost interest in my childhood hobbies.

I tried a cigarette once with some cider and felt so unwell, I actually was sick. I think this put me off cigarettes for life and for many years any kind of alcohol.

As years went by, I lost contact with many of the children I had known, as people do in different stages of their lives.

I suppose I could have made more effort; to be fair though, many of my childhood friends settled down very early in life, got married and had children. What would I have had in common with them now?

It's not that I did not want to meet anyone, I was just content and did not want to go out looking.

How would I have got on these last few weeks without Richard? Losing the closest person in the world and realising that for the first time in my life I am completely alone in a big empty house full of memories.

I know it's not healthy and I need to sort out Grandma's clothes for the charity shop, I know they cannot stay in the house. I am just not ready to erase her from my life.

Father Edward came to visit this morning and we agreed on the hymns and how we wanted the day to proceed. I cannot face doing a reading so Richard will read on my behalf.

Chapter 6

The Inquest and Funeral

The autopsy report concluded that Maud had died of a severe asthma attack. If Maud had been able to use her inhaler then she may have survived.

Sarah is still blaming herself for leaving Maud and keeps telling me that if we had not gone to London then Maud would probably still be with us as we would have been able to get the inhaler to her.

I try to get Sarah to see that even if we had been there the inhaler may not have helped; it was thought that it may have helped. Nothing was certain, though, and we must not blame ourselves.

The funeral was kept simple with few people attending, those being distant relatives, a few close friends and people from the local church. There would have been no more than 25 people in attendance.

Sarah had prepared a speech in memory of Maud; she had asked me to do this as she could not bring herself to stand up in front of everyone. I did this for Sarah, adding some words of my own, telling the congregation that I had not known Maud very long and that I wished I had known her longer as she was a very special lady. I even managed to shed a few tears.

Sarah had booked the local pub for the wake and had provided the first drink for everyone along with a cold buffet. She did not want everyone back at the house and with using the pub we could always leave when we wanted to.

We had gone straight from the funeral to the pub. I could see she was struggling, trying to keep talking to people and being polite without breaking down. I was relieved when Sarah said she wanted to leave. We made a discreet exit after just 45 minutes.

Chapter 7

Opportunities

I had not planned it but living in the house with Sarah provided so many more opportunities.

I took over the general running of the house, including the cooking and a bit of cleaning whilst Sarah tried to come to terms with her grief.

Taking over the household roles allowed me access to information I would not have known about.

Maud had taken care of all the financial aspects of running a home and Sarah had no idea of costs and monthly outgoings.

Deep in paperwork, drawing up plans for Sarah to see how she needed to account for things, I had access to all of Maud and Sarah's financial information, bank books, passwords.

I did the practical things such as advising the bank

of Maud's departure and set up new direct debits from Sarah's account, listing each item for her so she could see at a glance the monthly and annual outgoings.

We went through how to use the electronic banking, something Sarah had not done before.

Luckily the mortgage had been paid off some 20 years ago, and I was surprised and delighted to find that Sarah was quite a wealthy lady, in my view.

I had worked out from the paperwork and bank account that she had received a large inheritance from her parents' estate. Her bank account and ISAs came to just over £600,000.

The first week was a nightmare, getting Sarah to realise that she had to take charge of the financial things and that it would just not go away.

I suggested that in order to help, I could be added to her bank account as a joint card holder. The bank could not authorise anything unless I was listed.

We went to the bank and advised that we were living together, stretching the truth a little about how long I had lived there and before you knew it, I was a joint card holder.

Whilst Sarah was coming to terms with her grief, I was busy transferring money from our joint account to my own account.

I started with small amounts, chatting to the cashier about how I was paying for things direct as Sarah could not cope. I would then transfer that amount to my account, chatting about how this amount was for the undertakers or the house insurance.

To be fair, I was paying on my card and transferring the money although with some additional sums added to it.

The bank issued a statement to both of us each time a transaction was made. This was not an issue as I just made sure I got to the post first and shredded the statement. I had told Sarah all was managed online to help save the environment.

I did not take large sums until two weeks before we left for France. This would have been too risky. I had chatted as usual to the cashier and told her I was taking Sarah out to my place in Nice and that we were getting the house modernised whilst we were away. This story played out nicely as I could move larger sums for the new bathroom, new kitchen and carpets.

I managed to transfer £55,000 which is the maximum I thought I could get away with, after checking out general prices with online quotes.

I would have loved to have taken more but could

not risk being caught at this critical stage.

Chapter 8

Dala

Three months earlier

As she ran her tongue delicately round me, gently caressing me, I knew I could hold on no longer; as I ejaculated into her mouth, she pulled me into her, savouring the moment.

No other woman could make me feel this way. From the moment I met Dala she was the one for me.

We lay entwined as day moves to night. My time is nearly up, I must leave soon.

I have been seeing Dala for six months, costly at 100 euros an hour. I try and get to see her at least once a week.

Banging on the door, a voice shouts that time is nearly up. I quickly dress as she looks at me with those big brown eyes full of sadness.

"Take me with you," she pleads. "I just want you."

As I leave, a large Jamaican man enters the room. I am filled with anger and jealousy; I don't want anyone else touching my Dala.

Tracy is at the reception desk; we often have a chat since I come here so regularly.

Tracy cannot understand how I feel and has suggested I see another girl as I am becoming too attached. She has a young blonde, size six, that would see to my every need, new in last week.

I tell her that I only want to see Dala. Tracy shrugs and tells me to be careful.

I book my next visit and ask to see Ralph, the Operations Manager. I know from my visits that Dala has just over 150,000 euros to pay before she can leave.

She has told me this is the sum of money that Ralph and his friends say she has to earn, to cover the costs of transporting her here, accommodation, food and security.

For each paying customer, she accrues 50% of the money. She never sees the money; this, she is told, is looked after by Tracy.

She has worked out that it would take three years

to clear the debt, if Ralph ever does decide to release her.

If a customer is not happy then she does not earn anything, Ralph's idea of ensuring Dala does exactly what the customers want.

I have not got that kind of money to pay for her release; I work in the local supermarket stacking shelves. I stayed in France after first meeting Dala.

It was meant to be a holiday and I had booked three weeks off work to tour around France. I had never been that ambitious but had been doing OK, with my Grade 5 office job.

Dala changed everything and there was no way I was returning to the UK to my normal routine, never to see the woman I love again.

I had never had much luck with girls at home, they liked me as a friend and that was it.

I wasn't exactly blessed with good looks and being small, just over five feet seven inches, put the taller girls off. At work they had nicknamed me "Shorty".

Nobody missed me that much; Mum and Dad are in their 70s and currently on a cruise around the world.

I was never one for making friends and work wished me well on my journeys.

Dala had told me about her family and how she had ended up working for Ralph.

All she had wanted was a better future and to provide for her family.

Dala came from Romania and although life was not bad, she came from a large family and money was tight, especially with a younger sister with disabilities and her grandparents in poor health.

Her brother Mihai wanted to be a doctor and the family simply did not have the money to pay for him to fulfil his dream, attend college and all the other training that followed.

She had told me how wages are very low in Romania compared to the UK and that when promised a waitress job at a London hotel, getting paid £1,000 per month with accommodation, she had jumped at the chance.

Dala had been approached by an Englishman visiting Romania on business. She had been working at as a waitress at a hotel in central Sibiu and the man had left his card with her, saying he could help her become rich in the UK.

Dala met with him a number of times and he promised that he would organise her passport and travel and that the money she earnt in the UK would be sent back to her family.

He had even showed her photos of the hotel and smiling pictures of other Romanian girls working there.

Dala was shown video clips of girls telling her how great life was in the UK and not to miss this opportunity.

The opportunity seemed too good to be true and the only glitch was that she would need to pay back a sum of 42,000 Romanian leu which is approximately £8,000.

This would be done by instalments on a monthly basis at £250 a month over two years, eight months.

Dala signed a contract, showed proof of her current address; the only thing she was not happy about was being told not to tell anyone about this offer, even her family. If she did, the offer would be withdrawn. They said this was due to the risk to them fast tracking the passports and work permits.

It meant she had to leave without saying goodbye to her family and friends and not contacting them until she was safely in the UK.

This is how she ended up with Ralph. Unknown to her at the time, this was an organised gang, working across various countries to force girls into prostitution.

She had really wanted to tell Mihai that she was going on an exciting journey and would soon be able to help support him through college. She could not risk losing the opportunity though and consoled herself with the thought of him receiving the first payment from her work in the UK.

Dala had moved into a flat with Mihai a few months previously. Mihai had got her a job as a waitress at the hotel he worked in as a porter.

Money was tight but between them they managed the rent on a small flat within 20 minutes' walk of the hotel.

They both loved their family very much and were used to small spaces coming from such as large family. It was great them having independence and having a place of their own.

Their younger sister had become more demanding as her disabilities stopped her doing things she wanted to do and things at home had been very stressful for Dala which is why Mihai had found her the job over in central Sibiu.

Their family home was in Orlat, approximately 12 miles away, so not too far to visit and far enough away for them to lead their own lives. There were a few people at the hotel that had family near Orlat and they were happy enough to drop off Mihai and Dala en route when they visited their families.

On a wet Tuesday morning early February, Dala had crept out of the flat in the early hours without telling anybody, not daring to jeopardise her great opportunity.

Dala had not suspected anything was wrong until towards the end of the journey.

There had been six girls travelling together and they had been picked up just after 6am by a man called Marius in a large Transit van parked outside the public car park on the outskirts of Sibiu.

The journey was long and took just over 24 hours which included some breaks along the way. The girls had been told they needed to be seen by the minimum amount of people due to the risk, so breaks consisted of Marius issuing sandwiches and bottles of water with walks around the remote spots he managed to pull into.

Marius did not speak unless necessary and the girls had chatted amongst themselves.

It must have been about halfway through the journey that a new driver took over from Marius; Enzo did not speak much either and was keen to take the minimum of breaks and got cross when any of the girls needed to stop for a comfort break.

The first drop-off was in the early hours of the following day. Reveka was dropped off at a large country house with Enzo marching her out of the van. His explanation to the girls when asked why they were not all going together was that it was risky and so some of them would be split up. They wished Reveka good luck and continued to the next drop-off.

Mirela and Dacia had been dropped off at what looked like an old townhouse in a busy fishing village.

This had left Dala and the three others. Enzo had told them that the three of them would be taken to Nice, a place in France, and a man called Ralph would meet them.

Dala had asked how long it would take to the UK. Enzo had just smiled at her and said Ralph would explain everything.

As soon as they pulled up outside the large remote building, Dala had felt trepidation; something had not felt right and the other girls must have sensed it too as they had all gone quiet.

Two men had appeared next to the van, one Ralph and the other Michael. Enzo had told them to take all their belongings and said to the men, "All yours, nice doing business," had shaken their hands and said he may come over later to try a couple of the new ones.

Relia, one of the girls, had obviously felt something was not right and tried to run off. She did not get far and the man called Michael slapped her hard around the face and literally dragged her back to the spot she had been standing.

The girls were tired and petrified, the men were frightening and forcibly pushed them towards the building.

Inside the building, the man called Michael locked the doors and said that each of them had been allocated a room and they would be allowed to rest for four hours then they would meet with Ralph and be told what was expected of them and how to behave.

Dala had told him she had changed her mind and would find her own way back home. Ralph had laughed and told her that was not happening and that he owned her now.

Later that morning, Ralph had got the girls together and told them what was expected and what would happen if they did not behave.

They knew where their families were and bad things would happen to them if the girls misbehaved.

Ralph had showed them photos of their family and

their homes as a reminder that they knew where they lived and what they looked like.

"You will have customers and you will see to their every need and smile and make them happy."

Ralph told them that their first customers would be there this evening.

Alina, the youngest girl, probably no more than 15 years old, clearly did not have a clue what Ralph was referring to and looked at Dala for help. "I don't understand, what do we need to do?" Alina had asked.

Ralph had obviously found the girl's naivety funny and explained slowly and carefully that certain men would visit her, and she just had to do what they asked and smile and tell them how good they are.

Alina was still confused but was beginning to see what was expected.

Ralph told her not to worry and that he would see her first and show her what to expect.

That had been the start of their nightmare; from that day, the girls had not seen each other again and had been locked in separate rooms. Occasionally they had been allowed to go for short walks around the building on their own, supervised by Ralph or one of his men.

Chapter 9

The Plan

I have a plan. First I need to see Ralph and see if he will let me take Dala out for the evening.

I am not looking forward to meeting Ralph; he is over six feet tall and has muscles that look unnatural. Tracy said he spends three to four hours in a gym every day. He is not a nice man and can flip at the slightest word taken wrongly.

My courage is dwindling as I sit anxiously waiting for him in the little office next to reception.

Too late, he is here, striding in with an air of impatience.

"I hope this won't take long?" he demands.

I pluck up the courage and tell him of my plan to take Dala out for an evening, obviously with his permission, and that I will save up and pay the 100 euros an hour, totalling a large sum of 500 euros.

A big belly laugh erupts, as if he thinks it's the funniest thing he has heard.

"She is a whore, not a princess. You are a strange man."

"But can I take her?" At this point my knees are starting to shake.

"Why would you want to pay an hourly rate for that?"

"Please, I love her."

Now he is trying to keep a straight face, puts his arm around my shoulder and gives his verdict. "OK, if that's what you want, we are here to make our customers happy."

He agreed, although he issued threats and wanted security. I was to pay the sum of 500 euros upfront, the day before, surrender my passport (for safe keeping) until Dala was safely returned along with an additional payment on the day of 2,000 euros deposit. I would get the 2,000 euros back when she was returned no later than 11pm.

Although pleased with the result, how on earth was I to get that kind of money?

I have the sum of £1,200 left from my inheritance

from my grandad who died last year.

I am not a vindictive person; I hate violence and would never have hurt anyone. Life can change these things though, in order to help others and get what we want. Ultimately this is where it all started.

Chapter 10

Final Visit

My last visit to Dala before I start on my mission.

She runs up to me, pulling me into her arms, kissing me and dragging me towards the bed.

"No, Dala," I say.

Her face crumples and she looks confused. "Do you not want me?" she asks.

I tell her I want her more than anyone in the world, but we do not have much time and I need to go through a plan to get her safely away from here.

She looks uncertain and reminds me of a girl called Carla who had tried to escape. She had not got very far and was beaten to such an extent she could not eat for weeks, she very nearly died and still has the marks today given as a warning to others.

Ralph had been careful not to do long-term damage

to her face and chose to brand her arms with a hot iron, as a living reminder to never do the same again.

Each of the girls has been taken into Carla's room to see the extent of her injuries as a severe warning.

It is risky, although I am sure it will work, it has to. I explain to Dala that she will not be alone, I will be with her.

I go through the plan with her, explain how I could be away three to twelve months dependent on finding the right person.

Dala is excited at the prospect of coming to England, on a legitimate passport.

There of course is a risk and it is up to me to do my homework properly and make sure I get the closest match possible.

In the worst-case scenario, the immigration team would take Dala away, even this is a better than the position she is in now.

For me, I would do anything for Dala and if this meant going to prison then I would be happy to do so in the knowledge that she is safe.

So, I know the risks and consequences, which are not that great once in the UK. Here though, the consequences would be far greater and I will need to act quickly once I activate the plan.

I do not let my mind wander that far, thinking about what Ralph and his friends would do. I may not go ahead if I did.

Dala is reassured that either way, a life with me or picked up by immigration is the better option than the position she is in now.

I go through the detail as it's important to be honest.

I start with the planned night out, that I have already left a deposit for. How I will pick Dala up at 6.30pm. The exact date will need to be confirmed once I have a replacement.

Dala is to wear the clothes and shoes I will send in advance of the night out. I will have the replacement wearing identical clothes and shoes. I will try my best to make sure I get the right size, if I do not then Dala will need to adjust accordingly.

She really must practice her English; I provide her with a small language book I smuggled through. It does not matter about long conversations, just basic words to get by. I will say she is too upset to speak due to her dad having been taken into hospital.

Dala's English is very good, I just want it to be as

good as it can be to avoid any suspicion.

On the night I pick her up, I will take her to a small budget hotel and she will need to stay in the room until I return after 11.30pm.

We will then move over to the hotel I will be staying in. The replacement will at that point be gone.

Dala will take on the identity of the replacement and we will go straight to the room. I will get reception to order a taxi to the airport, explaining that we need to check out early due to my partner's dad having had a heart attack.

At the airport, we will book onto the first available flight to the UK, it does not matter where as long as we leave France. I know there are a number of flights each day so I feel sure we will get something. Even if it means time spent waiting in the airport lounge, we would at least have crossed one barrier.

During the flight Dala will avoid speaking to people and concentrate on reading a book or pretending to be asleep. I will keep to the same story, that her dad has had a heart attack and she is too upset to speak.

Once, in the UK, we head to a safe destination. At this stage I do not know where that will be.

We discuss how long it will take for them to realise we have replaced Dala. We suspect it will not be until morning, due to the time in the evening.

We cannot take any chances though, which is why when we go, we have to go quickly.

We have not discussed what will happen when they realise Dala has gone and a replacement is in her room. For us, we will have gone and that's the most important thing.

Time is nearly up. I kiss Dala goodbye, telling her to stay strong and that I will return as soon as I can.

Chapter 11

Return to UK

After arriving back in the UK, I needed to find some money quite quickly. The flight had cost £211 and with train and taxi fares I was now down to £460.00.

I had given Ralph 500 euros upfront before I left. I did not want him to later decide to cancel my evening out. I was also frightened I would run out of money, so paying the initial sum was the most important thing to do.

Mum and Dad would be away on their cruise for another four months; this left the coast clear to have a look and see if Dad still kept cash under the mattress.

Dad had always kept a couple of thousand for emergencies in the lining under his mattress, neatly stacked in small envelopes.

I was banking on the fact that old habits die hard

and despite modern technology, Dad would have kept to his traditional method.

The only people to be careful of are Terry and Pam, Mum and Dad's next-door neighbours and closest friends.

Lovely people but they are very nosy, always at the window, and if they knew I was back, I would be dragged in for tea and biscuits.

I decide to book into a local guest house on the Walliscote Road. They charge £30.00 per night for bed and breakfast. It does not look the best but it's showing vacancies and judging by the appearance of the property the owners should not pay me too much attention.

After checking in, I inspect the room – not great, very dated, some wallpaper peeling off, but it is clean and adequate for my needs.

Check-in was easy enough, basic form to complete and I paid in cash. The owner being a large man with receding hair called Alan, was preoccupied watching the match between Bristol City and Millwall on Sky.

I would wait until dark before going to Mum and Dad's place in Balmoral Way. Terry and Pam go to bed around 9pm so any time after that.

The journey to Mum and Dad's is just under three miles. I intend walking as it will help me think and to avoid meeting anyone I know.

I have plenty of time so I can take a detour and have a look down the seafront, see if anything has changed. I will then have an early dinner and coffee at McDonalds; I have really missed burger and chips.

An hour later after having had a couple of coffees and dinner, and read some of the local papers, it's nearly time to go to Mum and Dad's.

I slowly make my way across the streets of Weston-super-Mare; nothing much has changed, and people are still charging about doing their daily activities.

Tourists are walking up and down the seafront despite this being a cold day in early January.

From McDonalds it takes me just over one hour to get there. I had not rushed, there is no need.

Ideal, no signs of life, Terry and Pam's house is in darkness.

I make my way round to the back of the property and the garden gnome is standing in its usual place next to the back door. I feel under the gnome, and yes, the spare keys have been left in the usual place.

I have got a set of keys, I just needed to know that

the spare ones are there so that Mum and Dad will naturally presume they have been burgled.

I push the keys back under the gnome and use my own set, careful not to knock anything over and cause any noise.

Curtains are drawn with some lighting on, courtesy of Pam.

I make my way upstairs in semi darkness hoping to find a reasonable sum of money.

I know exactly where the hidey hole is – the bottom of the mattress, far right corner. I kneel down and feel for the opening. Yes, there are envelopes there.

I retrieve a total of nine envelopes, place them on the floor and start to count how much I have found.

A total of £9,000, a grand in each envelope. That's Dad, everything has to be precise.

I feel further in just to make sure there is no more, nothing, but £9,000 is a great start and I really cannot understand why so much money was hidden in such an obvious way.

Serves them right for not being more security conscious and it would probably be my inheritance anyway, so I am just having it early.

I carefully put the bedding back right and satisfied

the room is as I found it, I stuff the envelopes into my baggy jean pockets, ideal for carrying larger items, such as large sums of money.

I have a last look around my old family home. I don't know when I will be back, if I return at all.

In the lounge, I pick up a photo from the mantelpiece, one of Mum and Dad on their Silver Wedding Anniversary. "I am sorry," I say to Mum; she would be so upset, and it would probably take her quite some time to get over the burglary.

She is a private person and her home is her pride and joy. To think an intruder had been in would destroy her. I place the photo back in its position, kiss my finger and place it on her face. I truly am sorry and would never be doing this if it was not important; it is for the greater good.

I leave the house quietly, no trace that I have been. Nobody will know I have been until sometime after they return. This would be best, as I don't want to hear Mum crying on the phone.

I make my way back to the "Sunny Day" Guest House, wondering how best to start finding a pretty young woman, approximately five feet, mid-twenties, long dark hair, pale skin and around a size eight or ten.

Pretty tall order for a small man of just five feet

seven inches with no particularly striking features.

I have thought about dating agencies, speed dating, adverts in a local paper, online internet dating. All these would take time and be traceable one way or another.

After a long night of not sleeping well on the springy mattress and waking up thinking Dala was with me, I get up at 7am and think I have come up with the right action plan.

I pick up the pen and paper, helpfully left on the coffee table, and start working on my plan and associated costs.

I will need to invest some money in a car, get a map, buy some new smart-looking clothes. I will allow £4,000 and no more for the total investment.

At this stage I am unsure when I will get extra money and how long it will take to find a replacement for Dala.

It would be a disaster to run out of money, so I must act quickly and avoid unnecessary costs so that what money I have will last.

Breakfast is at 8am, a full English covered in grease and a mug of weak coffee. Not complaining though as it has given me good start to the day.

First stop will be at a local car dealership, older cars that have seen better days and I suspect in certain cases have been clocked judging by the mileage advertised for some. I had noticed this dealership late yesterday on my way to McDonalds.

The prices ranged from £800-6000, nothing that pricey here.

"Hi, I am Danny, can I help you?" a young man in a flashy shirt asks, within five minutes of me being on the forecourt.

I tell Danny I want a good-looking reliable car, good on petrol. I am not fussed what make, it mainly has to look good.

Danny shows me two cars that he thinks might be suitable, one an older style red BMW and a grey Skoda Roomster. The cost is similar. I am more interested in a discreet car that will blend in.

I inspect the Skoda; this is in good condition for its age. I can see no major flaws on the paintwork, and it is in reasonable condition inside.

At £3,200, it is slightly more than I wanted to pay. I offer Danny £3,000 cash if it test drives OK. Danny does not want to budge but eventually agrees a price of £3,100 with £30 worth of petrol.

For its age, just over 12 years old and with 35,000 mileage on the clock, the car drove well and was comfortable.

Danny tells me that the car will be ready in two days. I have to explain this is no good and I want it now to make a journey. I am not bothered about the car being valeted; it looks good enough to me.

As no other customer has turned up, Danny agrees to use his PC to sort out my insurance at the same time as doing the tax.

Danny sorts the tax and insurance out online, using the Compare websites; it makes the insurance thing so much easier.

I give Danny my mum and dad's address although I am hoping no post arrives for me. I have chosen the special online insurance which has no paper trail and tax will be paid for six months by which point my mission should be accomplished.

I can print off the insurance certificate at an internet café or library.

After two hours, I am ready to go. Danny had to deal with the odd customer in between sorting my insurance and tax.

Not sure where to head first, I think that I will

start to head north as I have not been further than Birmingham before and will keep driving and see where it takes me.

Chapter 12

Final Part of the Plan

Current time

Although things were working out well, Maud out of the way, Sarah's money being transferred to my account, I still needed to sort out what I would do once I got Dala back to the UK.

I don't know what they will do with Sarah over in France; they may keep her to pay off Dala's debt, get rid of her or release her.

I think that it is unlikely that Ralph and his mates would release her as they would not want to risk their business and Sarah turning up somewhere would spark a major police investigation.

Even so, I need to plan for the worst-case scenario of Sarah being released and the police getting involved.

If this happened, I would definitely be wanted man in the UK and might even appear on one of those Crimewatch programmes.

My passport would be traced to show I was back in the UK along with it showing that Sarah's passport had been used. My bank account would be monitored along with the car and the registration would be on the police database. I could soon be tracked down if I was not careful.

I had been thinking about this for a few days, how I could just disappear with Dala for a while without trace. I could think about longer term later.

It was through Maud that I came up with the idea. A small holiday flyer had arrived for Maud from a local coach company, promoting their trips to Scotland to small towns and villages with delightful scenery. The coach company was offering a week-long vacation for £350.00 full board.

I think this could be the answer and need to do some research. A nice, quiet, remote village.

Sarah came into the kitchen as I was reading the flyer, I quickly turned it over and said not to look as it was junk mail for Maud.

I had informed friends, family and companies of Maud's departure but every now and then a letter would arrive and Sarah would get very upset.

I tell Sarah I will go out to get the groceries so that she can look at the hotel I was thinking of booking on the internet.

I had told her that a short break to France would do her good and as my house was still being decorated we had best stay at a hotel until the work was complete.

Shopping list in hand, I head out, my first stop being the local library.

I pay the sum required to use the internet and start looking up Scotland and its hidden treasures.

I need to go as remote as possible. Inveralligin looks like one of the many good locations in the Scottish Highlands.

I discover that Inveralligin is a remote crofting township and that crofts (for food production) are established on the best land, and the poorer quality ground is used for livestock.

Inveralligin is situated on the north shore of Loch Torridon in Wester Ross.

A quick check on autoroute shows that it is just over 500 miles away from Grimsby which would take approximately nine hours to drive.

Definitely worth investigating, I decide to pay a visit to Inveralligin and see if I can book a cottage or caravan long-term. There seem to be plenty of these types of holiday lets available.

If I can secure something out of the way for six to nine months then it will give me some assurance for the short-term at least.

That evening, I tell Sarah that I have some business issues and need to go back to France for a few days. I am in danger of my snack bar being closed down, so I must get out there as soon as I can.

I tell her that there has been some trouble with some locals resulting in fighting in the street, other owners have been complaining and that I intend setting off tomorrow and getting a flight from Manchester. I will drive to the airport and leave the car in the long-stay car park.

Chapter 13

Sarah – Dependent on Richard

I know I have become dependent on Richard and the thought of him going away for a few days fills me with dread. I have also never stayed a night on my own before. Grandma was always there and even on holidays we shared a twin room.

I have not told Richard how I feel, that I will miss him terribly and that I will also be petrified being on my own at night and will need to sleep with the light on.

I hope he will not be away too long. He has booked a flight out to Nice and will book the return flight when he has sorted out the trouble with his business.

I wish I could go with him; I cannot do this as my passport has not arrived yet. I applied for it about two weeks ago. Richard has told me it could be up to six weeks before I get it.

There is plenty to be getting on with whilst Richard is away. I need to sort out Grandma's clothes and take them to a local charity shop.

I also need to really start giving the house a good clean. Richard has helped in the last few weeks when I was to grief-stricken to do anything; his cleaning though is not to the same standard as mine and what would have been Grandma's.

He has said he will call me when he arrives and not to worry if I don't hear from him straightaway as sometimes the signal on his mobile is not that good out there.

Chapter 14

Travel to Inveralligin

Nice and straightforward, Sarah waved me off around 8am, did not suspect anything, but then why would she?

I have planned out my journey and intend stopping after four hours for lunch and a refresher break and will then head on as far as I can go for about another three hours. I am sure I will find Travel Lodge, or Premier Inn that I can pull into and book for one night.

This will allow me time to relax and think about what I will say when I get to Inveralligin.

It will also give me time to relax and think about Dala and how we will soon be together without Sarah interrupting my daydreams.

I have chosen to drive; although it's an awful long

drive, it's the less risky option. If it all goes wrong, people might remember me on public transport, not that I stick out in any way but there is always someone that could remember me. Best to avoid other people at all costs and keep a low profile.

Chapter 15

First Night Apart

Sarah

Richard has only been gone 12 hours and I miss him so much. The house seems so empty, even with the radio on.

Outside it is dark and I am feeling frightened. I have locked all doors and windows, I did this when it started to get dark around 6.30pm.

I have also checked to make sure that nobody has broken in and is hiding in wardrobes. Not that it was likely, this being a quiet area and me having been in all day, but I needed to check as I am frightened being on my own at night for the first time in my life.

I am not going to tell Richard I checked in wardrobes, he would think it was really funny and may think I am weird.

I know lots of people my age live on their own and love it. I wonder if they felt frightened at first.

In the night, every sound seems magnified. The fridge must normally make the humming noise and the boiler makes a ticking noise, I just don't hear these noises in the day or when people are with me.

I will need to keep occupied. Having had dinner and watched some TV, I think about having a bath and going to bed early with a hot chocolate to help soothe my nerves.

Richard called four hours ago, just after 4.30pm, to say he had arrived and could not talk for long as the signal was not great.

He said he would be staying at a friend's house for the night due to the amount of dust in his house due to the new kitchen being installed. He will look for a cleaner to come in and do a deep clean before he moves back home.

He will call tomorrow probably later in the afternoon.

Bubble bath waiting, I double check the doors are locked and keep all lights on.

Richard

After settling in at a Premier Inn, I called Sarah and will not need to call again until later tomorrow.

Tomorrow morning, I have about another two hours' drive ahead of me.

I have given it a great deal of thought and if questioned, I will try and answer as honestly as I can, that my girlfriend is leaving home to be with me and that her family will not like it which is why we need somewhere remote for fear of repercussions.

I could say that her family had wanted her to marry her cousin and did not welcome outsiders.

It's as honest an answer as I can give. I cannot exactly say I have smuggled Dala to the UK and nasty people could be hunting us down along with the police.

Sarah

I feel dreadful, I must have had three hours' sleep if that. After my bath, I had gone to bed early. Every noise, small creak had made me jump.

I had turned off all lights apart from the landing light so at least I could see if anyone was there.

Every time I went to sleep I would wake with a jolt

convinced someone was in the house.

I even got up several times to do a complete check of the house.

I hope Richard is not away too long as last night was awful. Perhaps tonight I will sleep better as I am so tired.

Today, I will start sorting out Grandma's clothes and bag up for the charity shop; the cleaning can wait until tomorrow.

Richard

For Richard, it had been a great night's sleep. After the long drive, he had drifted into a deep sleep after having enjoyed a few beers and eaten in the hotel bar. Breakfast had been manic, with lots of families scrambling for tables; it was like the entire hotel had descended on the breakfast area all at once. After managing to find a small table, Richard had tucked into a large breakfast of bacon and scrambled eggs, looking forward to finding a place in Inveralligin for his future with Dala.

Chapter 16

Inveralligin

The journey took longer than he had anticipated, just over three hours, due to being stuck behind slow-moving vehicles and the sat nav losing signal.

He parks up on what looks to be a central parking area, £5.00 for the day. He can make his way on foot from here to see what Inveralligin has to offer.

The scenery is fantastic. Loch Torridon is surrounded by greenery and seems to expand endlessly towards the skyline.

There are long windy roads, with room for one car only. He wonders what drivers do when a car comes from the opposite direction, there seems no obvious place to pull in.

The are many waterfalls and lots of wildlife visible. The air seems much cleaner here. Despite being brought up by the sea, this air seems lighter and cleaner. Richard knows that Dala would love it here.

He imagines them going for long walks and picnics and not seeing anybody for most of the day. He could get them a bike each so they could go cycling.

He must have been walking around two hours, he is not even sure he is still in Inveralligin. Lost in day daydreams and with admiring the scenery, time has gone by.

It is then he spots what looks like a small caravan site in the distance. As he makes his way closer, he now realises these are what look like small chalets and not caravans.

There is a sign, "Private Property", and a smaller sign not far from it, "Accommodation Available".

The site looks to be empty, nobody about. Richard notices a house further up in the distance and makes his way towards it, thinking that there may be someone in.

*

Ross Campbell had been working out how to continue with the business – his wife Aileen had died of leukaemia three months ago – when a knock on the door disturbed him. Irritated, he got up from the table covered in paperwork and made his way to the door.

Aileen had been the backbone of the business, from the finances and advertisements through to the cleaning and meeting and greeting of the guests.

Ross just could not concentrate and even if he could he was not good with finances and had become resigned to the fact, he would need to sell up and move away from his home and business of 35 years.

It was not only the paperwork, it was finding someone that would work there, a part-time cleaner. It was so remote, not even one applicant had applied.

"No sales, thank you," he tells Richard, and tries to close the door. Richard quickly puts up his hand and tells him he only wants to enquire about renting a chalet for a long-term let.

Ross tells him they are closed and unlikely to re-open and so he cannot rent him a chalet long-term as he does not know how long this would be for.

This does not deter Richard who is insistent that even a few months would be good.

"What are you up to?" Ross is suspicious at how keen Richard is to rent a chalet on a site unoccupied.

Richard looks sorrowful and tells Ross he needs a secluded spot to go to with his girlfriend; her family are very religious and do not approve of their relationship, he fears harm would come to her if she remains in England.

Richard senses a slight shift in the man's stance and adds in hopefully that he would be willing to pay more than the going rate.

Ross could certainly do with the extra money. With no customers for the past six months he was struggling to pay the gas and electric.

When Aileen had become ill, they had taken no further bookings as she could certainly not look after the guests and Ross had spent all his time back and forth to the hospital in those final months.

The lad looked to be honest and seemed genuine about his reason for renting. He invites Richard in to discuss over a coffee.

"You will have to excuse the mess. Since my wife has gone, things are just not the same," he tells Richard.

Richard is shocked at the mess; papers everywhere, dirty cups scattered about and from his view of the kitchen it looked like a week's worth of washing up piled high.

Ross clears a chair and tells Richard he will be back

in a minute; Richard certainly does not fancy a coffee now but does not want to appear rude.

Coffee made, Ross gets to the task in hand and asks Richard lots of questions. He wants to make sure the lad is genuine.

Richard tells him about Lia, the love of his life, and how he intends to take her away from the bad home she lives in. He has chosen a different name as many people could be looking for them in the future and he thinks this a pretty name that would suit Dala.

He tells him of the father with the bad temper that regularly hits her, and how Lia's mother is so nervous she cannot leave the house.

He is frightened to leave her there any longer for her own safety.

The lies come easily, and sound genuine as the overwhelming love he feels for Dala shows in his expression and voice.

Ross is impressed that this lad intends leaving a good home and job for the woman he loves, with risk to himself. It shows he is a good person.

The conversation moves to Ross's predicament; Richard asked if he lived alone.

Ross does not like to share his personal business

with people, however, he has taken a liking to Richard and tells him a bit about Aileen and how they had run the business for years, and how he must cut his losses now.

Richard learns that there is a son, he went off travelling and never came returned. He does not even know his mum is dead.

The son called Aaron was last known to have been in America. There had been a falling out as he had wanted more money and Ross had refused to subsidise him anymore. He had been travelling for over 12 months, all paid for by Ross and Aileen. There had been no thanks, no post cards, letters and no phone calls until he had needed more money.

Ross had hoped that one day Aaron would take over the business; it was now clear his son was work shy and that dream had been shattered.

Richard has an idea which would be good for all of them and decides to put it to Ross.

The business can run again with Richard and Lia's help. Richard is good with finances and general administration, he tells Ross that Dala is good at cleaning – she looks after her family home as her mother is not in a fit state to do this and is also a good cook.

He has no idea if Dala can cook or clean, he just needs to get agreement so that they can live here.

Ross looks doubtful. Richard continues, saying they would not want payment, proper wages until things were up and running and money coming in. As long as they had a roof over their heads and enough money for food they would be happy.

Richard knows there is no point keeping on and that he should leave Ross to think about the offer rather than apply pressure.

He gets up to leave, touching Ross's shoulder, saying to think about it and he will come over later today before he heads back to England.

Once Richard has gone, Ross sits and speaks to Aileen. He imagines she is still there and asks her what she thinks.

Although he does not get a response – if he did, he would probably be frightened to death himself – he sensed her presence and that he should try and save the business with the lad's help.

Aileen had loved it here, meeting all the new customers and hearing about their lives and where they lived.

The business had all been her idea. At the time,

there had been little money to be made in farming and she loved being with people so when this land had come up for sale she had persuaded Ross to take a chance and do something different.

It had been a big risk but had paid off and over the years they had made a decent living.

Richard was hungry and decided to find a local pub for lunch; he had walked miles. He was careful not to lose direction so that he could make his way back to Ross later in the day.

After finding a small and friendly place for lunch, he enjoyed an extra beer, thinking he would take his time before going back to Ross. He did not want to go back too early and look over keen. The later the better would look best.

It was around 5pm when Richard started to make his way back to Ross. After lunch he had walked around admiring the views and checking for anything that might by a second option should Ross not agree.

Ross had been watching the pathway for the last 30 minutes; it was now 5.30pm and starting to get dark. Perhaps the lad had changed his mind.

Eventually, in the distance he spots Richard walking towards the house.

Richard apologises that he is so late and explains he took a wrong turn and was worried he had got lost.

That night Richard stayed at Ross's house; they had lots to discuss. It was dark and with no streetlights, Ross feared that Richard could get lost trying to find his way back to the car.

Richard helped Ross draw up some business plans and discussed the tasks that he and Alina could do, which ranged from cleaning the chalets, meeting and greeting guests, tracking of finances. This left Ross to do the jobs he enjoyed most, looking after the grounds and maintenance work.

Richard said it would be approximately four weeks before he could return with Lia; she would not want to leave before as it was her nan's 90th birthday coming up and she would not do that to her.

In those four weeks, it would allow Ross to put the grounds back in order and make sure all the chalets had been vetted and no work was required.

For the first time since Aileen had gone, Ross felt real hope and a glimmer of excitement at the prospect of the old site being up and running again. Aileen would be so proud.

Later that evening, Richard helped Ross clean up the kitchen and turn it into a fit state to be used.

It was no surprise that Ross had little food in, and they ended up having some tea and toast before bed.

Richard used what would have been Aaron's room, already made up waiting for the son to come home.

The next morning there was a much brighter and happier Ross; he would no longer be on his own and would soon be able to get himself out financially with the help of Richard and his girl.

Richard had told him he expected no payment until the business was making money and that he and Lia would be happy staying in the oldest chalet and would decorate to their own taste in time.

Apart from the chalet all Richard wanted was for Ross to provide food and had said he and Lia could pick up the shopping weekly for all of them.

Ross knew he would not get a better offer and he liked Richard, they had hit it off straight away and he like the sound of Lia.

Chapter 17

Holiday

Richard had returned from France on the fourth day, mid-afternoon, with a big bunch of flowers, telling me how much he had missed me and that he could not stay away any longer.

He had not managed to sort out all the issues and had to go back to France in the next two weeks and asked if I would like to go with him. We could turn it into the holiday that we had already been planning.

Of course, I jumped at the opportunity. I have dreamed of going to France for so long.

I had missed Richard so much and had literally been counting the hours until he returned. We had managed to stay in contact although phone calls had been short, and the signal had kept interrupting the line.

The second night he had been away, he had not

managed to get a mobile signal and I had been very worried about him. Awful thoughts had gone through my mind especially as he had not responded to my texts.

He had managed to call the next day, telling me he was only going to be away one more night and would soon be home.

I had been excited for weeks at the thought of going to France with Richard; he has told me so much about it.

I now have a passport, it had arrived earlier this morning. There was no point before, not having been abroad and going on holiday in the UK only. I would not have gone away without Grandma.

I have never been on a flight and I am petrified and excited at the same time. Richard suggested I ask the GP for some diazepam to help me relax on the flight. Evidently it's a common problem with anxious flyers and people happily take such things to remain calm.

The flight is just over two hours which seems an awful long time to be in the air when you are frightened.

The GP prescribed me a full pack with the strict advice not to drink alcohol with them. Richard laughed and said most people drink on the flight with the tablets as it helps to knock them out.

Every now and then I get upset thinking that I should not feel excited, I should still be grieving, although I know Grandma would be pleased that I am going with Richard and I hope she is looking down on us and seeing how happy he makes me.

Last week Richard took me on a special shopping trip for my holiday wardrobe. I now have a collection of lovely dresses and shoes with matching handbags. Richard insisted on paying for it all, saying it was his treat for his special lady.

In particular, I love the blue satin dress and matching blue suede heels; they show my figure off perfectly. Since losing Grandma I have lost a bit of weight and look better for it.

Richard has said this is my special dress for a night to remember. He will not tell me what he has planned but I can tell he is very excited.

I wonder if he plans to ask me to marry him. Will he propose on this night? He certainly has gone to a lot of effort and keeps telling me how he is looking forward to this night more than anything.

Chapter 18

Preparation

"Look at what has arrived for Dala." Tracy touches the blue satin dress and matching blue suede heels. "These are gorgeous."

Ralph looks up, uninterested. He cannot understand why Richard wants to take out Dala and buy her clothes and shoes. He has long ago given up understanding some of their customers.

It's like they lose all sense of reality and truly believe that what they have is love, choosing to ignore the fact that as soon they have gone, the girls will be all over the next customers, making them feel special and like they are the only one.

Tracy wants to know if she can give these to Dala.

Ralph does not see a reason why not, if that is what the customer wants.

He gives Tracy instructions for the planned evening out; he is not concerned although he wants to ensure that Dala is returned on time for the next customer.

This was not the first time one of the girls had been out for the evening, although usually, they act as hostess at a customer's home.

Sometimes, men wanted to create the illusion they had a girlfriend and others just want to show off in front of their mates that they either had a good-looking woman or let her offer services to his friends and business colleagues.

He makes sure that Tracy is aware of the deposit sum of 2,000 euros and the necessity for the passport for safe keeping. He had already received the 500 euros the day before Richard left for the UK. This had amused him no end, it was like Richard was so desperate to make sure he did not change his mind.

Tracy was told to remind Richard that Dala was to be returned no later than 11pm.

Ralph had booked Mr P in with Dala for 11.30pm that evening so it was essential that she was returned by 11pm to allow her time to get ready for the next customer.

Mr P was a mystery to Ralph; he came over on business on a monthly basis, did not talk openly about what business he was in and was always very impatient. He had been warned in the past about getting heavy with the girls. If they were out of order this was Ralph's department, certainly not a customer's. He wanted no marks on his girls, it was bad for business.

Although a strange character, Mr P paid very well and so Ralph was always keen to cooperate and work it so that Mr P had his choice of girls.

Tracy reads the enclosed note to Dala. "My darling, some items for you to wear on our special evening out, love always, Richard xxxxxx" Nothing worrying in the there, so she makes her way to Dala's room.

Tracy warns Dala to behave on the evening out and not to run off, as she knows what will happen. There is no escape and with no passport she has nowhere to go. A gentle reminder is usually all that was needed.

Once alone with the package, Dala reads the note with trembling hands. She had been practising her English at every available opportunity with the help of the small language book Richard had smuggled in on his last visit.

Not long now. Carefully she tries on the dress and shoes – they fit perfectly.

Chapter 19

Start of the Holiday

Sarah

Finally, the day is here. I could not sleep much last night, the excitement was too much.

Sun creams, insect repellent, shower gels have all been placed in my new green suitcase. Richard has said the airlines are very strict about liquids only going in the main suitcases and not the hand luggage. I have put just essentials in my hand luggage: my diazepam, hairbrush, mirror and wet wipes and my new book called *Perfect Chemistry* by Simone Elkeles.

Richard is going to drive to the airport and leave the car in the long-stay multi-storey.

Richard is very excited and tells me again, how I will love it out there and he can't wait to show me his house and beachside bar.

Richard had not slept well either, he kept mumbling in his sleep about how much he loves me.

I love him too, so much. I am in fairness besotted with him. I never thought I would meet someone as good as Richard.

He is funny, kind and caring. I have found that I enjoy sex. I had not known what to expect that first time and each time it has got better and better.

I am concerned about one thing though; Richard has suggested me doing things I do not feel comfortable with and has increasingly put pressure on me to try these things, telling me how good it would make him feel.

The other night he tried to force my head down onto him, telling me to open my mouth and he would do the rest. I just cannot bring myself to do this, it does not feel right.

He seemed a bit cross when I said I couldn't do it. We still ended up making love, although I sensed a lack of passion.

I have decided if it means that much to him, I will do it. Maybe when we are away on holiday, if I have a couple of glasses of wine, it may help relax me. The whole idea fills me with distaste but for Richard I will do anything.

He slaps my bum, "Are you ready?" He tells me he needs to pack the car so we can get there on time.

Richard

Finally, the day is here, I will soon be with my darling Dala.

Sarah is great, don't get me wrong. She is a lovely girl and in recent weeks has shown me a humorous side of her I did not know existed and sex has made progress and she is a lot less reserved.

I do forget at times, in the most passionate moments, that she is not Dala. I would have liked Sarah to have been a bit more adventurous, especially as each week, the nearer this day came I have become more and more aroused, thinking of Dala.

I keep thinking of Dala's lips around me, how I can thrust deep in her mouth. I did try with Sarah, but she would not even come near me in that way, quite disappointing. I pretend that Sarah is Dala, it makes me feel closer to her.

Last night I had vivid dreams about Dala and had woken up hot and frustrated.

I think Sarah is ready to go. Once the car is packed, we will be on our way.

I have planned for us to eat at the airport in the Frankie and Benny's restaurant; a glass or two of wine should help Sarah relax on the flight.

The last thing I need is any drama and Sarah being remembered by the cabin crew or other passengers or worse still refusing to get on the flight.

This needs to go nice and smoothly. Once, on the flight I will get her to take a couple of the diazepam. This I figure should knock her out for most of the journey and will give me chance to see the impact it has on her and how much I am likely to need for administration later this evening.

Chapter 20

The Flight

Richard

The journey could not have gone better. We had eaten at Frankie and Benny's with a nice bottle of Pinot Grigio and although Sarah was nervous, she bravely got on the flight with little fuss.

I had pre-booked our seats, extra leg room next to the fire exit, which meant it was just the two of us with no nosy person on a third seat to remember us.

I ordered us champagne, telling Sarah it was to celebrate the start of many holidays to come. For me it was a pre-celebration drink of what would soon be achieved if it all went according to plan.

Sarah was in the end so relaxed and slightly drunk, that she said she did not need the diazepam.

I managed to talk her into taking two tablets as the

effects of the champagne would not last for long.

Better than I had hoped, within 30 minutes of taking the tablets she was sound asleep.

Sarah

Richard had woken me to say we had landed. I did feel not right, very lightheaded and just wanted to sleep. Richard told me it was the effect of the diazepam; I don't think I will take them again.

The good news is that I am no longer frightened of flying. I was dubious about getting on the flight although I think I hid it very well from Richard. The wine with lunch had clearly helped.

I just need to become more alert so I can see all there is en route to the hotel.

Chapter 21

Arrival

There was lots to see en route to the hotel, lots of little bays and quaint houses dotted around the hillside.

With the sun shining and the rays bouncing off the sea, I like this place already and can understand why Richard talked about his other home so much.

It took just over 40 minutes to reach the hotel. Richard had booked a private transfer and the taxi man chatted most of the way, pointing out sights of interest.

The hotel is very impressive and has a gym, three pools, and spa facilities.

Our room has a balcony which looks over the Mediterranean Sea and we have a king-size bed with flowers arranged on top.

Richard told me it was only the best for me, and he intended to spoil me non-stop.

Richard has said he needs to go out for a couple of hours on business and that I could either use the facilities or have a rest. He is annoyed he has to go and says he will return as soon as he can.

I am happy to rest for a couple of hours and spend time relaxing and watching television before going out later this evening.

Richard has booked dinner in the A La Carte restaurant for 7.30pm. He tells me this is going to be a night to remember and to wear my special dress and shoes.

I hope he asks me to marry him, I could not imagine life without Richard.

Chapter 22

Plan Underway

With Sarah safely installed at the hotel, I make my way to collect Dala, flagging down a local taxi to take me to the outskirts of Les Adrets-de-l'Esterel.

I should be able to collect Dala, make the payment, have a chat with Tracy and check in at the second hotel by 7pm.

I had pre-booked both hotels the previous month for one night bed and breakfast for two. The five-star hotel is the one where I have used my real name, and for the two-star budget hotel, I have used a different name. This was a free reservation so no payment upfront was necessary. The great thing about this hotel is that it is only a five-minute walk from the first hotel which will make the transfer so much easier.

I cannot contain myself; the day is actually here; I have waited for this day for so long.

I get the taxi to drop me at the local bar and pay the driver a retainer of 20 euros to wait for me.

Tracy greets me like a long-lost friend; she has missed my visits. Being one of the few English-speaking customers it is not often she has chance to have a chat about what is happening in the UK.

I give Tracy the money, hoping she may forget to ask for my passport. It would make life a lot easier if this happened.

I get ready to go through to Dala, and she calls me back. Ralph has left a Post-it note on the desk reminding her of the need to hold my passport.

Not a problem, I have this with me, I just would have preferred not to have had the extra hassle later on.

She locks my passport and money in the top drawer using the key hanging from her necklace, reminding me at the same time that Dala needs to be back no later than 11pm, Ralph has been quite adamant on this.

I enter Dala's room. She looks fantastic, the dress fits like it was made for her. I am very proud and tell her how beautiful she looks.

She whispers to me that she is nervous. I hold her tight, reassuring her that all is in place.

As we leave, Tracy tells us to have a nice time and cheerfully waves us goodbye.

Outside, Dala takes a gasp and makes what seems a small cry. She tells me she has not been outside the complex since she arrived two years ago. Occasionally she had been allowed for a walk around the building with Ralph and his men watching. These times had been few and far between.

We walk slowly towards the taxi, holding hands in the early evening sun.

The taxi drops us at the second hotel just off the Promenade des Anglais in plenty of time. We check in as Mr and Mrs Griffiths. I know they won't believe we are married and will see me as another tourist with a girl for the night. I don't mind as Dala will not just be with me tonight but many more nights to come if all goes according to plan. I am one lucky man.

Once in the room, I quickly explain to Dala the plan of action and the need to be ready when I return.

I assure her that I have everything in place and have secured us a home and work back in the UK, in a place called Inveralligin in Scotland.

I tell Dala I must leave now. She tries to stop me, telling me she is frightened and does not want to be alone.

I hate leaving her like this, but I have to in order that the timing of the plan is not jeopardised.

I give her a long lingering kiss, and tell her to stay put, put a chair against the door and not open it to anyone other than me.

Very nearly time, just one more dinner with Sarah and then I can do the swap.

I let myself back in the room and Sarah is ready and waiting, in fact she is wanting more than dinner. She pulls me to the bed, telling me that tonight she will do whatever I want.

I cannot do this right now and need to ensure I don't cause suspicion.

I jump on the bed with her, sliding my hand up under her dress, lingering on one last touch. Nose to nose I tell her we can have all the time later, but we must go to dinner now as I have a special treat arranged for after dinner.

Sarah looks pleased and asks me what the surprise is. I tell her it wouldn't be a surprise then.

We make out way down the restaurant and are ushered to a table for two in the corner. A special request from me as I wanted the most secluded table for a romantic dinner.

The champagne on ice is already waiting.

We discuss over dinner the trips that Sarah would like to do, and I tell Sarah more about what Nice has to offer.

Sarah would like to do some shopping along Rue de France and visit Cours Saleya, with its colourful flower markets.

I have readily agreed to both and told her we can also take a walk up Castle Hill for spectacular views over the city and Bay of Angels. We could perhaps do this on our last day as something to remember.

We have just finished the main course of fillet steak with peppercorn sauce and now only have the dessert and coffee to follow.

I need to administer the diazepam now to allow time for this to work. I know that Sarah will need to go to the toilet shortly and wait patiently for this to happen.

I had on arrival at the hotel locked myself in the bathroom and ground down five tablets into the smallest amount of powder I could. This is now safely in my pocket to add to the champagne.

Sarah is already giggly, so this is the right time to administer.

She eventually goes to the toilet; I was beginning to think it would never happen.

No time to hesitate, I scan the restaurant; nobody is looking. I quickly add the powder to her glass and top up with champagne. I twirl the glass around to ensure a good mix.

Halfway through dessert and Sarah is slowly beginning to feel the effects. She has not mentioned feeling strange, I can see her eyes dropping.

I tell her I am off to the toilets and make my way to reception. I ask them to order a taxi to take me into town, I cannot risk hailing one down in case Sarah does not make it to the taxi.

Back at the table, I tell her it's time for her surprise. She smiles at me a bit lopsided and tells me she feels very drunk. She is slurring her words, not great, I must get her to the taxi quickly.

The taxi man is surprised when I give him the location, as it's not a tourist spot. I hastily explain I have some business to attend to.

Sarah is already asleep, her head on my shoulder.

Reaching what used to be my local bar, I pay the taxi fare and explain that my future wife has had too much to drink. Sarah is half awake and smiles up at me all dopily.

It is now 10.30pm, and I cannot mess up this final stage. I know that if I tried replacing Dala at 11pm, Ralph and his men would be there. They would not be back from the casino until then. I also know that Tracy will be busy checking out customers with some settling outstanding payments.

I try to get Sarah to walk with difficulty. I end up having to pick her up and carry her for the final three minutes of walking. Sweating with the exertion, I place her on the floor and tell her not to speak when we enter, as I am not supposed to let her into the business premises. I tell her to bury her face in my chest and I will help her to walk along.

She giggles, then half loses consciousness.

I enter the building, holding my breath. I am relieved to see that the reception area is packed. I shout over to Tracy that somebody has had too much to drink. Tracy nods and waves me on, shouting after me that I had better sober her up as Mr P, her next customer, is on his way.

I manage to half carry Sarah to Dala's room and open the door quietly. I don't want to disturb any of the other girls.

I quickly push the door shut with my right foot

and half drag Sarah to the double bed. I lift her up, she is a dead weight now, and I carefully place her on the bed and move her hair slightly over her face.

She is coming around a little, so I touch her face, tell her to lie still and quiet and I will be back shortly.

I quickly leave the room and make my way to reception. It is still packed full of people and I need to get out of here fast.

I wade in between the people and tell Tracy I have a taxi running outside and ask if I could have the money and passport. She throws me the key to the drawer.

Money and passport retrieved, I throw the key back to her and wave goodbye.

Outside, I run like my life depends on it. I loiter for a short while by the bar hoping to flag a taxi; there are none in sight. I continue making my way on foot, half walking and half running.

After what seems like an hour and in fact was only 15 minutes, I manage to spot a taxi and flag it down.

I must compose myself before I see Dala, things could not have gone better so far and I need to take deep breaths and calm down so that I do not mess things up at this stage.

I have done it; the swap is complete.

I ask the taxi to wait whilst I pick my wife up, handing him 10 euros.

Reception at the hotel is busy, so no need to make polite conversation with the receptionist.

I make my way to the room, knocking twice and telling Dala it's me.

She opens the door warily, worried I had changed my mind and had brought Ralph back with me to collect her.

I kiss her all over and tell her the swap has been successful and that we must go quickly.

I tell Dala to pretend to be upset, to lean into me and keep her face next to my chest.

Chapter 23

The Realisation

I don't know how long I have been asleep or where I am. I know that Richard will be back shortly, I hope he won't be too long.

I wake to find hands touching my breasts and can feel the firmness of him against my back.

"You came back," I murmur. I turn around slowly and in the semi darkness realise it's not Richard.

I start to panic, I cannot scream, no sound is coming out.

The man is old and fat and smells of body odour, I must be having a nightmare. I shut my eyes and pretend this is not happening. His touch gets harder as he prods me hard, twisting my breasts. It is at this point I realise this is no nightmare and is actually happening, I start to scream and this time the sound comes out.

The man does not like it and throws me back on the bed, hitting the side of my face.

"You know what happened the last time you played up," he whispers in my ear. I struggle against his weight, but he is so much stronger than me.

His fingers are now moving up my thigh; my screaming gets louder.

Before I know what has happened he has turned me over and has one hand over my mouth and the other holding me down. I cannot move with his weight against me.

He forces himself inside me, laughing whilst he does it. This is not like with Richard, this hurts and he is enjoying hurting me as he pushes in hard.

I wish I could lose consciousness, and this would be over. After what seems the longest time in my life, he has finished. He gets up slowly and tells me he will be back soon and that I must really learn to behave.

He takes his time getting dressed after using what I can see is a small bathroom. I consider trying to escape but know my legs are like jelly and I would not even be able to stand. As he leaves the bathroom, he takes a last look at me before turning abruptly and leaving the room.

I cannot move, I am in too much pain and I am shaking. I pick up the towel he has dropped on the floor and wrap this around me, crawling to the corner of the room in case he comes back.

Chapter 24

On the Run

By the time we get to the hotel, Dala is trembling from head to foot. I am frightened she might pass out and I hold her tightly, guiding her through the main reception area.

The receptionist waves to us and asks if everything is OK; it's pretty obvious it's not. I shout back above the noisy group loitering by the doorway that my girlfriend has had some very bad news and I will be back at reception shortly.

We really do not have much time. If we get caught now, all this has been for nothing and Dala and I could be in serious danger. I must get Dala to pull herself together.

I sit Dala down in the hotel room and speak patiently to her as I suppose I would do a child, choosing my words carefully. I stress the importance of trying to stay calm and acting quickly.

I show her the drawers and wardrobe that Sarah had placed the clothes in and tell her that she must start packing and that I will get her a brandy to help with her nerves.

She needs to get dressed in some of Sarah's casual clothes from the wardrobe and pack the rest of the items in the suitcase.

I place the suitcase on the bed and start putting items in to encourage Dala to do the same.

Back in reception I explain that Sarah's dad has had a heart attack and we must return to the UK straight away. I settle the bill and request a taxi for the airport.

The taxi should be 10 minutes and the receptionist has said she will call the room on its arrival to save Sarah waiting in reception.

On my way back to the room I pick up a double brandy from the bar for Dala.

Back in the room, I am pleased to see that Dala is fully dressed, including shoes and coat and it looks like all clothes and belongings have been packed.

Dala gulps back the brandy and ends up choking. I rub her back and tell her to drink it more slowly.

A check of the room confirms all is packed; I check my holdall and the passports are safely intact along with spare cash in envelopes, one in euros and one in sterling.

I show Dala the passport she will be using; it's the first time she has looked relaxed. She smiles and tells me she cannot believe how it looks like her. Picking up Sarah's handbag, I place the passport inside with the envelopes of money from my holdall.

I explain to Dala that nothing should go wrong but if it does and we get separated, she must go on alone, using the passport to get out of here. There is a total of £500 in each envelope which will be more than enough for her to get a flight and accommodation when she reaches a destination.

I know if we got separated that Dala would want to go home. I tread carefully here and tell her that no matter what happens she must not return to Romania as Ralph has people operating in that area.

The phone rings, the taxi is here, it's time to go. I grab the cases and holdall with Dala walking beside me clutching the handbag.

In reception, I wave and shout goodbye to the receptionist. Dala has her head down as instructed just in case anybody spots she has changed.

The taxi journey took just over 30 minutes and we were silent the whole journey, both too excited and anxious to speak and for me the fear that the driver would know Ralph.

The airport is crowded and I did begin to think we may not get a flight. Luckily there is a flight to Newcastle in 90 minutes' time and we can have the last two seats.

Tickets paid for, we check in our baggage and show our passports, all OK so far. I was never too concerned about the first check as it's only someone on the baggage desk looking briefly at the passports, it's the next stage I am more worried about. Still a good start.

We make our way to the security area, the risky bit. Dala knows if we get caught here she must tell them what has happened to her and that the police must be called.

It's always been a risk but a risk worth taking. Either way, Dala is now out of Ralph's hands.

I hand over my passport and boarding card first, go through without looking back at Dala, trying to act as normal as possible.

I so desperately want to look back but join the queue for the hand luggage scanner. I feel someone next to me and look up with relief to see Dala. We have done it; we will have just one final check before we board.

Hand luggage going through the scanners, I walk through the body scanner. Dala copies what I have done and follows behind me.

We pick up the hand luggage and do not speak until we are in the lounge area.

As soon as we are through, I take Dala in my arms and give her a big reassuring hug and whisper to her that the hard part is done. One more check before boarding and we should be clear.

We have an hour to spare so we sit down in a quieter area of the airport, content just being together.

The flight is called, the final check is about to happen. I am frightened of it all falling apart on this final check but will not let Dala see this, just another 30 minutes and we could be in the air.

We go through with no problem; the flight is packed and we went through the final check with lots of families and unruly children, ideal for us.

The flight is noisy – there is a stag party on board, causing havoc. I could not have wished for better, it meant that nobody would be paying us much attention.

We are two rows down from the stag party of about 20 men.

After a rowdy flight, we land in Newcastle, just one last check of the passports. I know out of all the checks this is the trickiest being in the UK, with the additional problem that the French authorities may have alerted the UK if they know about Sarah.

The risk has always been there and just to have Dala free would be enough for me; she knows that the police in the UK will help her. I would be arrested, there is no doubt about that, but this is a small price to pay for Dala's freedom.

The Captain tells us to remain in our seats and at this point, what looks like airport security board the plane. My heart sinks, this is it. "I am so sorry," I whisper to Dala.

As they walk towards us, I get ready to leave with them. There is no point in arguing, there is nowhere to run and after all I have done a number of crimes and must now pay the price.

I get up to say that I will not be any trouble, but they walk straight past us towards the end of the plane. I twist my neck round to see what is going on.

They are taking a middle-aged woman off the flight. I wonder what she could have done.

I can't believe my luck; I just hope for no more close encounters. I really had thought that was it, my luck had run out.

We passed through the airport with no problems.

My legs feel now like jelly; I am just so relieved and in shock that we are actually here, safe in the UK.

I know we must keep moving regardless of how tired we are. As soon as the authorities are aware, then the police will be looking for us. I am also not sure as to the extent of information that Ralph could get hold of. How many people work for him? Would he know we are in Newcastle?

I had done some prep work before setting out for France and I know where we need to head and have some knowledge of local hotels.

One of the nearest train stations to Inveralligin is Aviemore; my plan is to get us safely to Aviemore, stay at a local hotel and get a taxi the next day from Aviemore to Inveralligin which will take just over two hours.

The train journey is long at just over five hours. I cannot sleep as there are three changes to make en route and I need to keep alert just in case people are after us.

I let Dala sleep; all the stress has taken its toll and she had fallen asleep within 20 minutes of being on the train.

Chapter 25

The Swap Is Known

"Right, all done here, I had better check on the girls before I go." Ralph asked if there had been any problems. Tracy tells him there were no issues apart from Mr P was not happy and said Dala had been very awkward.

"This is what happens when we let customers take them out, they come back thinking they deserve much better." Ralph's brother Michael had never been happy with the girls leaving the premises, thought it left them in a vulnerable position. He would have them locked up 24/7 to avoid any risk to their reputation and profit.

"What happened?" Ralph asks. Tracy tells him that Dala would not let Mr P near her; he had to issue a few slaps to bring her in order.

Tracy checks on each of the girls, leaving Dala until last. She may need to have a quiet word. Dala has a cushy number with Richard and she needs to remember that.

She pauses at Dala's door, thinking, *Better get this done with*. As she enters the room she wonders where Dala is then spots her sat huddled in the corner of the room wrapped in a towel.

Switching on the main light she walks towards her, something is wrong.

This can't be happening. What is in the corner of the room is not Dala, this is another girl, shaking and frightened to death. She has blood coming from a gash on her right eye and bruising starting to appear on her left cheek.

"What' s your name?" Tracy asks softly.

All she gets in response is, "Help me." The girl is shaking non-stop with tears running down her face. She starts to speak in stutters "There was a man, he did things to me, he has hurt me, I tried to stop him." All goes quiet then she asks, "Where is Richard?"

Tracy strokes her hair and tells her she will be back shortly. The girls grabs her, begging her not to go in case the man comes back.

Tracy tells here the man has gone and she will go and look for Richard.

Tracy locks the door after her; she cannot risk the girl running out the room.

She finds Ralph and Michael watching a video they have made with the new girl.

"This will be a best seller," grins Ralph, "look at her going for it."

Michael realises something is wrong. "What's up, Tracy?"

"It's Dala, she has gone, there is another girl in her room."

Ralph has had too much to drink and laughs, telling Tracy she must be imagining it.

"It's true, the poor girl in that room is petrified."

"This cannot be happening. How many times did I say, keep them in?" Michael looks furious and asks Tracy to take him to the room. He does not go near the girls himself so has no idea who is in what room or even what most of their names are; he likes to stay at arm's length and let Ralph do the day-to-day running of the business. They make their way to Dala's room with Ralph following behind, convinced that Tracy has made a mistake.

Tracy unlocks the door and the men stare astonished at the sight in front of them. The girl starts crying, telling them to stay away and that she will tell Richard.

Michael tells Tracy to tidy her up and strides out of the room. Ralph lingers a while longer, wondering how this could have happened. How that little prick could have pulled a stunt like this.

One thing is for sure, he will hunt him down and make sure he gets a lesson he will never forget. Ralph is not a man to be messed with.

First things first, they need to decide what to do with girl and find Richard and Dala.

Ralph and Michael are still discussing the best way of dealing with girl when Tracy returns.

Ralph is getting increasingly annoyed and asks Tracy how she could not have noticed. Tracy tells him not to blame her, she was busy at a peak time with customers when Richard had returned with the girl, who was a very good lookalike and was wearing the same exact clothes and shoes.

"What was I meant to do, stop dealing with the others and go and inspect Dala?"

"I take it he has his deposit and passport?" Michael asks.

"Yes, he took them from the drawer."

"How long has he been gone?" Ralph wants to know.

Tracy recalls he arrived just after 10.30pm and left 10 minutes later.

"We need to find him fast," Ralph thunders. Michael and Ralph are already making their way out.

"What about the girl?" asks Tracy.

"We will deal with that tomorrow," is Michael's response. He tells Tracy to make sure the girl is locked up and to go home, they can decide what to do in the morning.

The girl looks up hopefully as Tracy enters the room. Tracy tells her she has to go now and will be back tomorrow.

The girls makes a run for the door; Tracy blocks her way. "Sorry, love, you need to stay here tonight." Tracy forces her back towards the bed, tells her to be quiet and not to annoy the men otherwise there will be big trouble.

Tracy quickly leaves the room, feeling sure the girl will do as she is told.

Chapter 26

Hunt for Richard and Dala

Ralph and Michael had hunted for Richard throughout the night; they found that he no longer rented the room above the supermarket in which he had worked.

Pierre de Villiers told them that Richard had given him a few days' notice back in December and said he would not be returning. There was a new lad doing his job and renting the flat.

Pierre de Villiers had not been best pleased at them turning up late at the supermarket; he was still busy cashing up and they had frightened him, barging in like they owned the place.

They had asked him where Richard would be likely to be. Did he have any friends? He had told them he knew nothing of Richard's life and that the lad had seemed a loner.

The man called Ralph had give him a business card with his number on with the instruction to call him if Richard appeared or if he had any information that would lead them to Richard. Either way, he would receive 500 euros if it led to Richard being found.

Pierre de Villiers knew better than to ask what they wanted with Richard, although he did wonder as Richard had seemed a quiet, genuine lad. Probably drugs, that was what everyone seemed into these days.

They searched the late-night bars and restaurants in the hope they would find Richard and Dala.

They checked with the staff in almost all of the local restaurants and bars to see if anyone matching Richard and Dala's description had been in that evening. They left business cards with the promise of a reward if they received information which would lead them to Richard and Dala.

Ralph was getting more worked up as time went by and at 4am they called it a night and made the phone call to warn Mihai. The call they had been dreading.

The news had not gone down well; Mihai had been very cross and asked what sort of establishment they were running, just letting girls walk out when they felt like it.

Mihai had started up this business and had been

very successful.

He relied on men like Ralph and Michael to keep the girls secure and minimise potential risks. He now had stakes in places like this in several different countries.

Getting rid of his sister was a bonus. She had been nuisance, always going on about looking after the family and how they should do more.

He had made sure she got the job at the hotel so that she could become an easier target.

For him, he just had to talk about how he wanted to be a doctor and how he did not think he could ever do this due to their family and money situation.

She had turned out to be a good earner, one of the best. For each girl, he received 20% of the profit. Far better than a doctor's salary.

He would have her back there in no time, she would be sure to come running home to tell him what had happened.

He told Ralph he would be in contact when she returned home as he felt sure she would, and he would personally see to it that she was returned as soon as she made an appearance. In fact, he would bring her back himself.

Mihai no longer stayed in touch with the family. It was all for Dala's benefit, to show him in a good light. A visit must be made soon though in case she turned up at the family home.

"Did you find them?" was Tracy's first question the next morning.

Ralph and Michael tell her that there have been no sightings whatsoever and it's like they have just vanished.

Michael is going out shortly to visit local taxi firms to try and establish their movements.

"What about the girl?" This has been on Tracy's mind all night, locking up an innocent girl who had gone through a dreadful ordeal.

Michael wants to use the girl to pay off Dala's debt. "I won't have it, it's wrong." Tracy has never gone against Michael before but cannot allow this to happen.

Ralph asks her what she would do, adding sarcastically, "Perhaps let her out and wave her on her way directing her to the local police?"

"She could ruin our business and blow the entire operation," were Ralph's final words.

The only other option they had thought about was to give the girl a heroin overdose and discard the body out in the countryside.

They give Tracy the final choice as she is so worried. "What's it to be then?" asks Ralph. "Do we keep her and put her to use or do we get rid of her?"

Tracy tells Ralph that the girl would be better off dead and that the heroin overdose was the kindest option and the right thing to do under the circumstances.

They agreed they would do this later when they could transport her more easily under the cover of darkness. In the meantime, the girl would be given a hefty shot of the heroin to knock her out.

They make their way to the room; the girl had been waiting and tries to make a run for it. Michael blocks her way and pushes her back into the room. "On the bed," orders Ralph.

The three of them hold her down as she screams and struggles, kicking out aimlessly.

Ralph quickly produces the syringe and administers, thinking it was a good job it was early morning and no customers were about yet.

Michael is thinking, *What a further waste of money, using the good stuff on her.*

They don't like using heroin on the girls as they

pride themselves that their place is one of the few in which most of the girls are clean. Nothing worse than a girl covered track marks and over time they look old and haggard quickly.

The stash they keep is for the girls that use it as unfortunately some girls will just not behave and need the heroin to calm them down, and secondly make them work for their money for the next fix.

It does not take long to get them addicted, sometimes less than a week.

The girl loses consciousness and satisfied, they leave the room. Tracy locks it anyway just in case; they cannot risk any further surprises.

Chapter 27

Tracy

Tracy had not slept much the night before, four hours minimum. She had not been able to get the girl out of her mind.

It was one thing the daily business but a young girl from the UK that was meant to be here most likely on holiday was another thing.

Who was she? Her family would be looking for her, the police might be informed.

It was mainly the look of absolute fear in her eyes, total shock at what had happened, and her asking for Richard.

How could he have done something so bad? Even in Tracy's standards this was absolute madness.

Had Richard and Dala left the country? Were they still here in France?

Tracy knows that Ralph and his men will hunt them down either in this country or the UK. They have many contacts across a number of countries.

She had not known what to do and at 4am had packed her small amount of belongings and placed them in the boot of her car along with what money she had and her passport in case she needed to make a quick getaway.

She had never liked the new girls being broken in and had for a large part avoided the girls until they had become more accepting like Dala.

It was an agreement with Ralph and Michael that she would never be around when the new ones arrived; she could not bear to see their faces, frightened, their dreams shattered and worse still the cries and screams. Michael in particular could get very rough with them in order that they behaved from the offset.

How many times had she had to bathe a black eye, bandage up broken fingers and in some cases had to stitch the odd wound that would not heal?

The bad part had never lasted that long as the girls soon quietened down after Ralph or Michael had taken them in hand, and those that did not behave within the first week were so high on heroin they were oblivious to what was happening around them.

Tracy had worked for the boys, as she called them, for 10 years. Although what they did was wrong, they treated her well and she quite often saw them as the sons she did not have.

Any problems she had, they sorted. She was never short of money and any gambling debts were put right or a nice quiet word was had with the person or business she owed money to.

Tracy was 42 years old and had once been a happily married woman, working as a nurse in Birmingham.

Tracy had longed for family and this had never happened; after four miscarriages she knew it was not meant to be.

She had become depressed, especially as friends and family were at the stages in their lives that babies and christenings became a mainstream subject.

Terry had wanted children too and it was awful seeing his face each time she miscarried. Once, she had gone four months and he had started to get the spare room ready, painted it blue and white with little teddy bears attached to the wall. He was convinced it would be a boy. After that, they never spoke about babies again.

Tracy started going to bingo, playing online poker, anything that would keep her mind active and off babies.

Within a year, things had got out of control and Tracy was not even going into work half the time and used to call in sick as she just wanted to go to the casino, arcades, anything that involved gambling.

Tracy had run up debts of over £56,000. Terry was mortified when the bailiffs had come knocking at the door. He knew she had a problem but had not realised how bad.

They had ended up having to sell their home and downsize to a two-bed semi in an area Tracy would previously not have considered.

Another year later, the marriage could not take the strain and they divorced, Terry stating the reason as unreasonable behaviour, listing the gambling and debt.

Tracy moved out of the semi as she knew it was all her fault and was the right thing to do. She had moved in with another nurse called Becky who had a spare room to rent.

It was cramped with the three nurses in one small house, but it worked financially. Sally mainly did nights in ICU which helped, as three women using one bathroom was a nightmare.

She had managed to hide the extent of her

problem at work and only her closest friends and colleagues knew.

One day, she had no more than £2.82 left in her purse for the week. She had nobody she could ask for money, so when the opportunity arose at work she felt she had no option.

It was an elderly lady, very posh, and she was in A&E after a bad fall. Tracy was to stitch up her arm.

The lady had needed the toilet; Tracy had helped her to the cubicle and said to knock when she needed her.

It had all happened so quickly, the handbag left on the chair next to the bed with the purse sticking out.

Tracy had quickly opened the purse, taking out a wad of notes; it was unfortunate that Doctor Evans had drawn back the curtains as she was doing this.

Tracy had been escorted from the building and knew she would be given the sack.

The shame of it, all the other nurses staring.

She could end up going to prison. How could she have sunk this low?

The police officer and Legal Aid representative had been very nice considering what she had done.

Terry had paid her £500 bail; he still cared for her

and was shocked at what had happened.

He had driven her back to Becky's, begging her to sort herself out.

Tracy knew Becky would not want her living there anymore, why would she? Who could blame her? She would never trust her again.

There was nothing left, she would certainly get the sack, it would be all round the hospital by now and she may get a custodial sentence.

With no money, no job, no references, no family to care for, what was left for her?

The only thing she could do was to disappear, spare Terry further embarrassment and pain.

She was not going to get far on less than £3.00, so it was with great sadness she raided the savings pots in the kitchen. There three of them added a contribution each week for the rent, gas, electric, water and council tax; £480.00 in total. In the least it could get her a flight somewhere and then she would see what work she could pick up.

No idea where she was going, Tracy hastily packed her bags, called a taxi and set off for the airport.

She would start a new life somewhere that nobody knew her.

That's how she had ended up in France, a cheap flight for £89.00 setting off within 90 minutes.

Ideal, before people realised she had gone.

The money she had taken had not lasted long and she had been down to the last £20.00 when Ralph had come to her help in a local bar.

She had been on the verge of being thrown out after arguing about the bill, after a few too many gin and tonics. She had not been thinking straight and had lost track of how much money she had spent.

The room she had rented was above the bar, so it was convenient just to come downstairs for some food and drink.

She had been the only English person staying there so with nobody to talk to she had ended up having few more drinks than normal.

After getting a taxi from the airport, she had been unsure where to go and had asked the taxi man if he knew of any cheap accommodation in a secluded location.

As luck would have it, his uncle had some rooms available on the outskirts of Nice, nothing special but clean and basic, for 35 euros a night. Tracy was more than happy to book in for the week whilst she figured out what to do.

As the taxi man had said this was definitely a secluded area, which is what Tracy had needed, also to give her time to try and conquer the gambling problem.

Unknown to her at the time, the bar was a meeting place for local businessmen of rather dubious characters.

Ralph and Michael had watched her since her arrival a few nights previously. Michael was sure she was on the run, definitely on her guard. Ralph had been suspicious that she may have been an undercover detective. This suspicion had gone after witnessing her losing her temper with the bar attendant and threatening to punch his lights out.

Ralph had decided it was time to introduce himself. He had intervened, settled the bill and point blank asked why she was there and who she was running from.

Tracy had tried running, thinking the police had found her. Michael had blocked the entrance, so she had no choice but to speak.

After she had told them the truth, admitting she has fled the UK and had no money, she expected them to either arrest her, if they were the police, or keep as far away as possible.

Instead, Ralph smiled and said he had a proposition for her.

That's how it had all started. Ralph had dressed it up, saying it was an establishment visited by high-profile clientele and the girls were well looked after. They were expanding and could not manage on their own.

They needed someone like her to manage the books and reception, all above board.

In return they would pay her rent, basic wage and look after her in general as long as she brought no trouble to their door.

If she betrayed them, she would not see the UK again. This threat had been made twice and Tracy knew she would be a fool to cross them.

She wondered now, if the threat still applied after the years of loyalty she had given them.

All good things must come to an end and she knew that for once in life she had to do what was right.

She could not leave that poor girl there to the mercy of Michael and Ralph with their many customers that would enjoy taking a vulnerable girl.

She was sure that Michael would not go along with

the plan of giving her an overdose and would persuade Ralph to put her to use and get some money out of it.

Neither the lethal overdose nor keeping the girl here could she live with.

There was nothing for it, she would have to do right by the girl even if it meant she herself could come to harm.

She tells Ralph she is going to check on the girl as she does not want to be mopping up vomit and dealing with hysterics later on.

Ralph tells her not to be long as he is on his way out shortly to sort out some business over at the bar.

Tracy quickly makes her way to Dala's room.

The girl is starting to come around. Tracy makes sure the door is locked behind her and half drags the girl into the bathroom, starts to undress her and turns on the shower; nothing like a bit of cold water to help bring her round.

She gently slaps each side of the girl's face, shakes her and tells her she will help her, but she needs to try and pull herself together so that Tracy can help her.

The girl says she feels sick and will try and do what Tracy asks.

Tracy tells her that they need to act quickly and

that the drowsiness should soon ease.

The girl is nodding, trying to get her body to move although the coordination is not great, courtesy of the hefty heroin dose.

Tracy tells her she has 10 minutes maximum to try and pull herself together and be dressed and ready by the door.

Tracy sorts through the solitary drawer containing Dala's clothes, finds a t-shirt and leggings, picks up an old pair of trainers from beside the bed and gives them to the girl, telling her this is her only chance and not to mess up and to stay quiet until she returns.

Back in the reception area, Tracy's heart is beating rapidly. She feels nauseous and faint at the prospect of being caught. She dreads to think what the boys would do if they caught her.

Ralph gives her a kiss goodbye and tells her she is the best and that he should not be long.

With Michael already over at the bar, Tracy is alone in the building. She could release the other girls but decides it is too risky and that she is doing more than enough helping the one girl. After all, she is the one putting herself at risk.

She takes the money from the petty cash box; no

time to count it but she knows that there are roughly 500 euros. The boys have never been stingy when it comes to looking after her or the customers.

She needs to move fast, before she changes her mind.

The girl is ready and waiting although still stumbling about. She is slight in build so Tracy is sure she can manage to get the girl to the car.

Tracy locks the door behind them and moves as quickly as she can towards the car park with the girl clutching on to her arm and almost dragging her down.

It's like carrying a dead weight. Eventually after what seemed like 10 minutes, they are at Tracy's car.

"I really need you to help me by pulling yourself into the car," Tracy urges the girl. One final push and she is on the back seat and seems to have passed out. Tracy is not worried about this, as long as they get away.

Shaking from head to toe, Tracy starts up the car, no time to change her mind now.

It will take longer but far safer to go the back route and not pass the bar; it would be just her luck for the boys to spot the car.

Tracy has driven for 30 minutes and will soon be

at the police station in Nice. She knows she cannot just pull up outside as she will probably be caught on camera. She will get as close as she can and the girl can make her own way from that point.

The girl is starting to come around. Tracy starts speaking to her and tells her they are near a police station and that she cannot go in with her and she will need to go in on her own. "Can you manage that?" The girl nods and tries to speak but no words come out.

"When I pull in, you must leave the car straight away, ask for help to the main entrance."

Tracy pulls in slowly; the girl looks at her one last time and clambers out of the car.

Tracy accelerates away as quick as she can, not wanting to risk anyone remembering her car or registration.

She had formed no plan other than to get to the airport and try to get a flight somewhere. Spain would be nice as it's warm and there would be lots of work she could do in the holiday resorts.

Tracy would be happy working in a bar or café, just as long as she had enough money to live on.

It felt good having helped the girl. It had been a

long time since Tracy had put anyone else first.

She wonders if her passport will be flagged as a "wanted person". It would be more likely in the UK rather than Spain as she is not exactly the high-profile criminal. It's a chance she will have to take.

Tracey knows that things may catch up with her eventually and she could face a custodial sentence for attempted theft of the elderly lady, skipping bail and stealing money off her flatmates.

She will face it if it happens, in the meantime, her one aim is to get as close to the airport as she can, dump the car and get the next available flight out of Nice before the local police find any link between her and the girl.

Chapter 28

Alone in France

―⊙⌒

Sarah watched as the car sped away. She felt awful, pain in every movement and her vision was blurring.

If she can just manage the few steps she could get to safety. The woman had said this was a police station.

It was too much. After a couple of faltering steps Sarah collapsed near the kerb leading to the front door of the station.

It was a couple passing that spotted the figure lying across the pavement; they alerted staff in the station and between them and a police officer they managed to carry Sarah inside.

Sarah had woken in hospital a couple of days later. The nurse explained how she had been transferred to them and had been sedated due to her injuries and state of shock.

Sarah tells the nurse she had been held down and a man using a needle had put something in her arm. The nurse assures her she knows and Sarah has been given medication to counteract the effects.

As she becomes more alert, Sarah starts to panic, looking to see if those men were there. Such was the scale of her panic, her heart rate and breathing increased to such a rate that she had to be sedated again.

It was not until four days later that Sarah was able to explain to the hospital and police what had happened and that she thought she had been kidnapped and that Richard would be looking for her.

An interpreter had been brought in and worked with the local police to piece together what had happened.

A check with the hotel she had stayed confirmed that a Sarah Potter and Richard Smith had booked in on Wednesday 22nd April and that they had left the same evening due to an emergency at home.

Hotel staff were able to show the police the CCTV of them arriving and leaving. It was when the CCTV was being shown to the police that the Hotel Manager, Mr Berger, spotted that it was not the same woman leaving.

The women were very similar, almost identical,

especially in the footage from earlier that evening showing the ladies dressed for dinner.

The difference was that the woman that had checked into the hotel had a two-inch scar on her right hand, not really visible but caught at an angle under the security light it stood out. She was also very slightly smaller in height, perhaps half an inch.

The police had thanked the hotel for their help and checked with passport control if Sarah Potter and Richard Smith had left the country. Their worst fear was quickly confirmed, that they had left country on Thursday 23rd April.

The British Embassy were informed of Sarah's predicament and the need to contact Sarah's family, provide her support following her horrific assault and ultimately organise her travel home including a replacement passport.

Based on the information that Sarah had been able to provide, the police had pieced together a rough picture of what had happened.

It appeared that Richard Smith had used Sarah's passport to take another girl out of the country.

They believed that the girl may have been a prostitute and Sarah had been returned in her place, looking identical in the same clothes.

Mr Smith had gone to great lengths to ensure the two girls had looked almost identical.

What was a mystery was why Sarah had been taken to what was presumably a brothel. Could Mr Smith not just have taken her passport?

Sarah had taken the news badly, not believing that Richard would do such a thing. She told them of his business and house, how he must be kidnapped too.

It was not until the British police had confirmed that money had been taken from Sarah's bank account that she would believe them.

Sarah had given the police full authority to check her bank details, after police had ascertained Richard was a joint account holder; they had wanted to try and track him down to find out what had happened.

She could still not fully believe what had happened, how Richard was not the Richard she knew and loved. He had used her, stolen her money, had her raped and beaten and now there would be a separate inquest into Maud's death, as Richard had been the last person to see her alive. He could have killed her beloved grandmother.

The hospital had run tests to make sure she had not picked up any sexually transmitted diseases, she was receiving counselling and would soon be home in the UK.

Sarah had been warned that appeals would be made on the news, in order to try and locate Richard and the unknown woman.

Sarah had provided photos of Richard taken from their trip to London.

How could she have been so trusting? It was embarrassing having to admit to the police she knew nothing of his family or where he had lived previously. She had been so naïve. In some ways Sarah did not want it on the news; she did not want people to know how stupid she had been.

The counsellor told her that Richard had deliberately set out to con her and men like him were quite accomplished so she must not blame herself.

Why could she not have seen him for what he was? Why on earth had she shared her bank account with a stranger? How could she not have noticed he was using her? All these questions keep going round and round in her mind.

Then there is that man, the things he did to her, unnatural and laughing as he did it. She can still feel him, smell him and no matter how hard she tries she cannot get the images out of her mind.

She has been told in time, things will get easier. Sarah doubts this and cannot see herself ever being able to move on.

How could Richard, the man she had loved, have done this to her? Lying, taking her money, planning such deception at the same time as smiling and telling her that he loved her.

How could he have just taken her virginity like it was nothing?

Telling her what a special evening was planned, the dress the shoes, he must have known what would happen to her. How could anyone be so cruel?

The Support Officer had just been to see her and delivered further bad news.

It had now been confirmed that Maud had likely been suffocated; the second autopsy had shown signs of suffocation by direct force.

The previous autopsy had not picked up on some minor details as there had been no suspicion around the death.

Richard was now wanted on suspicion of murder as well as kidnap and theft.

"How could I have been so stupid? I am so sorry, Nanna," Sarah sobs into her pillow, inconsolable.

Chapter 29

Lia and Richard Taylor

I was really pleased with how things had gone according to plan. After the long journey to Aviemore we had managed to book in at the hotel I had looked at on the internet a few weeks beforehand.

It was old and tired-looking and not many people staying. Near to the local shops, it was the ideal location.

Last night, going to sleep with Dala was a dream come true. We had made love until the very early hours until we both were exhausted and fell into a deep sleep until the daylight woke us around 8am.

Room service had been a must with buck's fizz with our breakfast to celebrate the start of our lives together.

We have not got long until we check out of the

room, so I start out on my shopping expedition.

We need outdoor clothes, the type that I have seen people go hill walking in – backpacks, waterproofs, trainers, sunglasses, scissors, hair dye and I had better get a hairdryer, I don't think the hotel has one.

I also have the letter to post to Dala's brother. Dala had written a letter last night to tell him what had happened to her and to be careful of Ralph and his men.

Dala does not have a telephone phone number for him as Ralph and Michael had gone through the girl's belongings and taken anything such as mobile phones and address books, so they could not contact home.

Luckily Dala could remember the address. She can only hope that he will receive the letter.

No forwarding address has been included in the letter or even our whereabouts as we cannot risk being found.

Letter posted and shopping complete in under an hour, I walk happily back to the hotel with heavy bags.

It's a dreadful shame that Dala will have to cut her beautiful hair. I know it will grow back, it's just I love Dala the way she is. Last night I had run my fingers through her hair for the last time.

I hand her the scissors and hair dye, a nice deep red colour. "I won't look like me," she says. "You won't recognise me." I tell her I love her, hair or no hair, so even if it all goes wrong she is stuck with me.

Dala laughs and tells me I will see a new her in 45 minutes.

Dala knows she has a new identity when we get to Inveralligin and we have agreed to start using the new name from today. Fortunately Dala likes the name Lia.

For me, I will still use the name Richard, but I will now be Richard Taylor.

Whilst Dala is transforming herself, I shave my head. I have never done this before and have always been rather proud of my thick brown hair. It has to go, though; we need to look as different as possible.

I switch on the television whilst waiting for Dala, checking on the news. All well there, just the mention of swine flu and the increase in reported cases.

"Are you ready?" she shouts. "Close your eyes."

She has grabbed hold of my hands and tells me to open my eyes slowly. "Is it really you?" I ask.

She looks fantastic; the short choppy cut in deep red really suits her, a complete restyle. "I think I will be taking Lia to bed tonight instead," I say, twirling her round the room.

Dala inspects my head and spots some hair I have missed and shaves off the remaining bits, telling me my head will now get cold.

We clear the room up, carefully packing the hair dye container and Dala's hair in the side compartment of Sarah's suitcase, careful that we do not leave any evidence. We can get rid of these when we get to Inveralligin.

It does not take long and we are ready, in our outdoor clothes, ready to face the world as Lia and Richard Taylor.

Chapter 30

Life in Inveralligin

The journey to Inveralligin had been quite nice, lovely scenery and the sun was shining.

We had told the taxi man we were touring the UK and were keen to experience the great outdoors for a longer period of time than our usual two-week holiday. We had taken time out of work to allow us to travel at our leisure around the UK for a full six months.

The taxi man was quite chatty and happily told us all about Scotland and places to visit.

I got him to drop us off a five-minute walk away from Ross's place just in case there was ever any suspicion. I did not want to lead the police directly to our hideaway.

Dala – I must start referring to her as Lia, no slip-ups, even in my mind I need to adjust to the new name – is taken aback at how lovely it is here.

"It is so pretty, and calming." She flings her arms around my shoulders, jumping up to kiss me, making me drop the cases. I fall slightly backwards, holding her tight and give her a long lingering kiss.

I tell her that I hope she will be happy in her new home and that I will do my best to make sure she is never hurt again.

Ross was pleased to see us; he had been delayed in getting the site ready due a bad cold and was starting to get worried that I might have changed my mind or arrived much later in the season.

Ross and Lia took to each other straight away and we settled into life at Inveralligin easily.

Those first few weeks were very hard work, up at 6am daily to try and get things up and running. We were all asleep by 10pm as we had worked non-stop for 12 hours a day.

We had to work hard to make sure that the site was up and running ready for the summer period.

Lia was brilliant and made sure we had a full breakfast to start the day with and rounds of drinks throughout the day.

As each chalet was complete, Lia then started the

full clean; it was a bit like a conveyor belt. Ross would do his jobs, I would complete mine then Lia would finish up.

I was grateful that Ross was kept busy as I had been on the news several times. Fortunately, with the swine flu outbreak and the parliamentary expenses scandal taking priority on the news, I had managed to avoid Ross seeing me on the television.

It was on the seventh day of being in my new home that I was first shown on the news. It was the early evening news; Ross had been having a shower at the time.

I had not been on screen that long but enough for Ross to have recognised me. Despite having shaved my head, he probably would have put two and two together.

Sarah must have given the police the photo from our trip to London; it was a picture of us standing outside St Paul's Cathedral. I had been careful to avoid photos being taken, but before I knew it, Sarah had asked a passer-by to take a photo from her mobile.

The news was brief and to the point. I was wanted for kidnap and suspected murder, my accomplice and I were considered highly dangerous and not to be approached, there was a number on the screen for people to call.

It had gone on to say that the girl in question looked like Sarah and could herself be in danger.

The reporter appealed to the public for help catching the suspects, outlining what had happened to Sarah, who had been raped and beaten during a 48-hour ordeal.

So, they knew about Maud. I suppose that it had only been a matter of time before they had looked at this.

I had hoped, if the kidnap business had come out, I would have got away with the Maud thing and been able to appeal on the grounds that I was rescuing Dala. With murder though, I would be locked up for a long time.

I had not realised that Lia – I always refer to Dala as Lia now – had entered the room and she asks me, "What have we done? That poor girl, I thought they would have realised." Lia sits down, visibly shaken.

I had already explained to her about Maud, with some added bits, saying she was very unwell anyway and had limited time to live so in essence I was putting her out of her misery.

Lia wants to know what we should do. I tell her

that we are just to continue as we are and keep Ross away from the television.

I take Lia to get the food shopping so we can just forget the newspaper. We don't need to go out for a few days anyway, we have enough food in.

We are so busy anyway; he will not have time to put on the television.

Dinner is almost ready now and we generally sit around the table talking after dinner. I quickly switch the television off before Ross makes an appearance.

Lia has tears in her eyes and tells me she had not wanted another woman to go through what she went through.

I tell her we had no choice and that Sarah is now free and will be looked after by the police and support groups.

I would not have wished any harm on Sarah either. I had no choice though, I had to leave her there in order to get my passport back, I would have been hunted down in no time if I had stayed in France.

There had always been a chance this could happen, in fact, it could have been worse, they could have kept Sarah a prisoner and used her to pay off what would have been Lia's debt or killed her.

I am surprised they let her go as this was a big risk to them and there would have been no way she could have escaped from a locked room. Even if the door had accidently been left unlocked she would never have been able to get past the reception area unnoticed.

As Lia finishes off the dinner, Ross asks me what is wrong; it was clear Lia was upset.

I tell him that today is her sister's birthday which is why she is upset. Ross nods his head saying it's understandable and that perhaps in time Lia may be able to contact her family again.

Chapter 31

Lia

I love life here; I feel safe and secure with Richard and Ross although I will always have part of me that will remain sad for my loss.

I miss my family and know I cannot return home or to get in touch with them. This could mean us being tracked down by the police or Ralph and his men.

I also don't want them knowing what has happened to me, it would break my parents' hearts and I would rather them now think that I had just run away, it's better this way.

Mihai may tell them at some point, if he gets my letter. For me though, it is better that they are spared the pain.

Sometimes I think about the girl called Sarah and what she went through. Because of her I am now free.

I will always be very grateful to her; if it was not for her, I would most certainly still be locked up, having to deal with men from various nationalities that knew my predicament but did nothing to help me.

They would have kept me there until I was of use no more.

What she must have gone through was terrible, waking up in a strange place, having someone attacking her, no place to run and later the realisation that Richard had done this to her. She must have been so confused and frightened.

I too had been raped and beaten until I had learnt that it was better to do what they wanted as they would do what they wanted to anyway.

I had lost count of the number of customers I had to service, how many times I had to pretend I enjoyed being with some of the most disgusting men.

I hope she has people to help her move on and that she does not get the reoccurring nightmares that I do.

Richard tells me it is a small sacrifice that was made for greater good, meaning my freedom. I am sure Sarah would not see it that way.

All I had ever wanted was a better life for my

family and as a result I was forced into the sex trade. Sarah became a victim and Richard committed serious crimes to help me.

A part of me will always grieve for my family, the precious time lost, the fact they may think I just abandoned them.

I will never get the chance to tell them again how much I love them and I would do anything for them.

I don't let Richard see my grief; I hide this from him. He has done so much for me and would be upset to think that what we have is not enough to fill this hole in my heart.

The truth is no matter what Richard did, nothing could ever fill the gap of losing my family.

Each year, I will place flowers down by the beach in memory and in hope that my family are well and that maybe by some chance we will meet again.

Chapter 32

10 Years Later

Sarah

I am still having counselling although I am down to a one-hour session once a month.

I now teach at a local primary school. I have always liked children; the counsellor had said six months after that terrible time that I needed to focus on something in order to help me get better.

When Grandma was here I was occupied. I found with her being gone that I had a lot more time which meant more time thinking about what had happened.

Training to become a teacher had kept me focussed, from obtaining my degree through to the teacher training including helping out as an assistant at the local school.

The children taught me how to laugh again, how

to begin to trust people, although I don't think I will ever fully trust anyone again.

What happened to me will scar me forever. Even now I cannot come to terms with how Richard could have been so cruel. To purposely set out to find someone that he could use, take what he could physically and emotionally, not caring what would happen to me after.

How could he have just taken Grandma's life, ending it just because she was looking out for me? She had really cared for Richard and must have been so frightened in those final moments.

I had since found out that Richard came from the seaside town of Weston-super-Mare. He never had distant relatives near my home village, he did not have a home or business in France, in fact he had worked in a local supermarket there.

The police believe that he had also stolen from his own family. Whilst his mum and dad were on a cruise they believe that he had taken the remainder of their life savings from the family home.

This could not be proved, however, sightings of Richard had been confirmed in Weston-super-Mare; a hotel owner had come forward to say he thought that Richard had stayed at his family-run hotel.

Richard's car had been bought at a local car dealership and records showed the date tallied with the hotel stay.

He had never picked the car up from the airport, I suppose the intention was just to leave it all along.

The money he had stolen from me had probably been used to help with their planned escape and pay for a place to hide.

The police are not even sure if he is in the UK; there has never been any tracked movement from his bank account, passport, no CCTV footage, it is as if he has completely vanished.

Richard had taken cash from his personal bank account at various times before we went away, the final withdrawal being the day before the holiday.

He had planned everything in fine detail. One line of enquiry was that he had used the money for fake IDs.

I often wake up at night wondering what he is doing. How can he live with what he has done? I also think of the other girl; does she know about me? How Richard used me to help her? How did she end up in what the police believe was a brothel? Are they living happily ever after?

I absently touch the scar on my right hand; this was something that Richard had not taken into account. It was from a horse-riding accident when I was younger. I had fallen at a three-foot jump during a dressage competition. It had faded over time but would always be there as a reminder.

I am told that the other girl was almost identical to me and it was only the scar that had showed the difference in us and the slight variation in height. They do say that everyone has a double somewhere. I wonder if she still looks the same or has changed the way she looks.

The French police had done a thorough search of the local area and had found no such operations in the distance I had travelled.

The distance covered had been extended up to a 50-mile radius as I had been so unwell at the time, I may not have been fully aware of the true travelling time.

They had found an old farmhouse which looked like it had been left in a hurry, with clothes, cigarettes and alcohol left behind. It was likely this had been the brothel.

The building had been rented and all leads had come to an end when it emerged that the person who had rented the property had been deceased for over

20 years. Each lead that the police thought they had came to an abrupt end.

This means that the gang could be operating elsewhere, they have got away with what they did to me and nobody will be made to pay for what happened.

Father Edward has said that I must try and forgive Richard, that I will feel better after forgiving what he has done. He is not the one that has been through what I have, how can anyone forgive what Richard has done?

I am a good Christian and it hurts me that I cannot issue forgiveness, I just simply cannot forgive him for what he has done to me and for what he did to Grandma.

I am meeting Peter tonight for dinner; Peter works at the school with me and knows about my past.

We meet once a week on a Saturday night. Peter would like to go out more and knows that it will take time. He is very patient and understanding.

We have been seeing each over for just over a year and have got as far as holding hands and a kiss goodnight. Peter has said he will take things as slowly as I like and has offered to come to the counselling sessions with me.

I know I am slowly getting there with trusting people again, although my trust will never be like it was before.

Peter is a good man, he has worked at the school for over 15 years. I have met his parents and even joined his family for Christmas dinner. They have all been very supportive.

As the counsellor said, I must not let one man ruin my life; there are bad people out there and equally I must remember there are good people, I just need to let people into my life to see this.

Ralph and Michael

It was a very costly experience. We had to leave the establishment in hurry and getting the girls organised for the transfer had not been easy.

We had to set up a whole new customer base at the new establishment, a 10-minute drive from the centre of Marseille.

Mihai had organised the transfer and we had concentrated on getting the girls out quickly.

We had luckily received a call from a customer who had told us that the girl was called Sarah and that she was in hospital after ending up at the local police station.

She was unconscious and would be for a couple of days. Nothing could be done due to the police presence; it was too risky. This meant we had to leave within the 48 hours. Mihai had been furious.

To think that this all came about because of the short guy from the supermarket, it had made him a laughing stock amongst his business people.

If ever he got his hands on him, he would kill him very slowly.

Michael blamed him for being far too trusting. From now on things were done Michael's way – no external visits or trips out, no matter what price the customer offered. It was far too risky.

The new establishment was doing nicely, and they even had some of their old customers come over for a visit.

Mihai had warned them that if anything like this happened again they would be on their own; he wanted maximum money made with minimum hassle.

He wonders where Tracy is. He still cannot understand how she could have done this to them.

Tracy would not have messed about and would have gone straight off after taking the girl. They had found her car not far from the airport.

They had looked after her, gave her a chance when nobody else would, and this was how she had repaid them.

He hoped she was OK. Despite what she had done, he did genuinely care for Tracy.

She had been like a mother figure at times, looking after them. They had never had this before, their own mum having been a drunk and on the game.

They had covered for their mum when questions had been asked about their care. After all, she was their mum. She had died of liver failure on Ralph's 16th birthday.

Their dad had left when they were young. Ralph and no memory of him whatsoever and Michael being slightly older could vaguely remember him.

Michael being the older brother had taken care of him, as he had done most of his life.

Michael had been determined to have a better life than his mum had lived and had started out in the sex trade very early on in his life.

Being a good-looking boy, he had easily got the local girls to do what he wanted, making it all sound perfectly normal.

After a year Mihai had called it a day looking for Richard and Dala. There had been no trace of them whatsoever, they had even been on the news and the police were after them. It was too risky to continue the search and a year later they could have been anywhere.

On the news, it had said that Richard was wanted for murder. To think that Richard was capable of such a crime, they had definitely underestimated him.

They knew that they had made it to the UK as Mihai had received a letter from Dala.

They had been convinced that Dala would have been back in touch with Mihai, but no contact was ever made.

Maybe Richard had killed Dala too? Realised she was not what he thought?

He had certainly misjudged Richard. He would not make the same mistake again, the embarrassment from this episode was enough.

Tracy

Tracy lies back on her sunbed, thinking just another 30 minutes then she would need to go home and get ready for work.

The busy beachside restaurant that Tracy works

for caters mainly for families, offering a large variety on their menu and fixed-price offers.

Tracy loves life here; mixed shifts mean she can have plenty of time out in the sun. The beach which is a 10-minute walk from her flat is in a lovely secluded location, not a beach that the tourists often find unlike the main one near the restaurant where she works.

It was by chance she had ended up here. After getting a flight to Barcelona she had managed to get a late-night bus which ran direct to the town of Sitges.

She had simply hopped on the bus and decided to get off at what looked to be a busy resort with numerous night spots.

It had not taken Tracy long to find work, literally two days. She had spotted a sign in the restaurant window: "Waiting staff required – no experience necessary".

It was Day 1 that Tracy had seen the advert and on Day 2 she had the interview and started work that evening.

Joey, the restaurant manager, had said two of the young girls had left without notice to work at a nightclub down the road.

It was a large venue and many of the staff working there were youngsters. This did not bother Tracy and she had gladly accepted the job.

She had managed to find the small flat whilst out walking one day and negotiated a sensible rent, it was just as well that she had come across it when she did as her money had soon started falling rapidly after paying for the flight then a hotel for two weeks.

The wages at the restaurant were not great, although there were two good things: firstly they paid her in cash, and she got to keep any tips on top. The second was that all food and soft drinks were included as part of the employment offer.

This was ideal for Tracy who still had a gambling problem and if left to her own devices would have had no money left for food.

She was more sensible now and made sure that the rent was always paid upfront. She knew she was lucky to be here and may not get a chance elsewhere.

Tracy considers she has been very fortunate; things could have turned out very differently.

She was glad she had helped the girl; she had not done many things to be proud of and this at least was one thing she had done right.

She could not put right the wrongs that had already been done to the girl, but she was responsible for having ensured the girl's freedom.

Tracy had followed it on the news, discovered the girl was called Sarah, watched the appeals. She was not surprised that Richard and Dala and not been found, as she knew only too well, if you wanted to disappear you could with either careful planning or luck and opportunities which is the category she fell into.

She was happy enough to spend the rest of her days in Sitges, there were far worse places.

Ross

I consider the day that I met Richard to be one of the luckiest in my life. It was like fate had stepped in and brought us together.

After losing Aileen, I was about to give up. Everything we had worked for would have been for nothing.

For months after Aileen had gone, I had got more and more depressed, I had let the house and site fall into decay.

Richard was the first person I had seen in over a month.

I could not face going into the village and the local shopkeepers offering their condolences. They meant well, I know that, I just could not face it, it was like admitting that Aileen would not be coming back.

I don't know what would have happened to me if Richard had not turned up that day.

It came as a shock when I found out the truth about Richard and Lia. I did not find out until 12 months after they arrived.

It was early one evening, I overheard one of the guests' children telling her mummy that the man in the paper looked like Richard.

The parents had studied the paper and told the child that lots of people look like Richard and that the man in the paper was a bad man wanted by the police.

They had left the paper on the bench they had been sitting on.

I had picked up the paper out of curiosity and was shocked to see Richard listed as a dangerous man, wanted for kidnap and murder.

He had been one of 12 people listed as part of an annual appeal for Britain's most wanted criminals.

There had been a brief summary, detailing how he had smuggled a girl back to the UK using a stolen identity and the victim whose identity had been used had suffered a 48-hour ordeal in France, having been raped and beaten. It had gone on to say, he was also wanted in connection with the murder of the girl's grandmother.

I did not know what to think; it certainly looked like Richard and it was around the date that he had arrived here.

In a state of shock, I hid the paper under my jumper and returned to the house for dinner.

I managed to hide the paper under the wardrobe so that I could look at it properly the next time Richard and Lia went shopping.

I had to wait six days until Richard and Lia went on the weekly grocery shop. I knew they would be gone about for just under two hours.

As soon as they left, I got out the newspaper and retrieved Aileen's old laptop from the bottom of the wardrobe. She had said to keep it as a spare in case the new one broke.

Aileen had bought a new laptop shortly before she became ill; this laptop had become very slow and running a business, she needed things to work quickly and had not wanted to take a risk and lose all the important information such as the guest bookings and financial accounts.

Richard did not know about this laptop, so I could browse the internet without causing alarm.

After 10 minutes, I knew all there was to know. I knew beyond doubt that Richard Smith was Richard Taylor and Lia was Dala.

The photos, the timeframe, the girl called Sarah that could be Lia's double.

This was why Richard had needed a secluded location.

I quickly turned the laptop off and placed back in the wardrobe. I did not want Richard and Lia to know that I knew the truth.

I thought back over the last 12 months. The time I had nearly cut my finger off whilst trying to fix the unstable wooden table, Richard had been insistent on taking me to the hospital to get it seen to.

That first winter, I had come down with flu, Richard and Dala had looked after me; they had each taken turns and had not left my side, changing the bed linen and making sure I drank lots of fluids.

The fun we have had playing board games, going for walks, the odd evening out at the local pub.

I realised that I loved Richard and Lia like they

were my own son and daughter.

The paper and various news articles had made Richard out to be a dangerous, ruthless person, this was not the Richard I knew.

There was no doubt it was Richard and what he had done was wrong.

Love can do strange things to people and I know without doubt he only did what he did for Lia, or should I say Dala. It had all been for Dala.

He is not the monster that was portrayed in the news; the Richard I know is kind and caring.

I knew then that I had to make sure that Richard and Lia would be secure once I was gone.

Aileen had made me promise that no matter what, we would leave all of our money and estate to Aaron. I could not break that promise, although I could make provisions to ensure that Richard and Lia remained safe and secure.

Two weeks later I went into town with them and visited my solicitor. I amended my Last Will and Testament so that they could remain in Inveralligin for as long as they wanted.

My dying wish was listed; that they remained running the site. If the business had to be sold, they kept the chalet as their home and inherited a third of the estate, listing in the Will, that they had input cash into the business when I had been in financial difficulty.

My son is ruthless when it comes to money and would have put up a fight if I had just left Richard and Lia a sum of money. This way there could be no argument.

Richard and Lia were too polite to ask what I had been doing. I offered no explanation.

I have written a letter to Richard which explains what I have done and why and that I knew the truth, that I understand and will love him and Lia always.

Richard will not see this letter until I die. It is safely in the hands of the solicitor and will only be issued after my death.

I hope that they will have many happy years together and enjoy the business as much as I did with Aileen, and that I get to enjoy a number of these years with them, before I join my beloved wife.

Richard and Lia

The last 10 years have been the happiest of my life.

Life on the complex is great. We see guests mainly

from March to September and in the winter months we may not see people for months on end, unless we go to the nearest town to get food shopping or go for a meal at the local pub.

It can be hard work at times, keeping the now busy site up and running properly, but we are happy doing this as it's rewarding and we know we can take time back for us in the dark winter months.

Lia is a natural with the guests, they love her and there any many regulars that come back year after year.

She takes such pride in getting the chalets ready and nothing is ever too much trouble.

Angela and Pete, our close friends, had been regular guests, had been coming here for six years, then they decided to retire and make Inveralligin their permanent home.

We go out once a week with them; usually on a Friday evening we go for dinner or a game of snooker at the local pub.

Sometimes Ross will join us, mainly if Lia has talked him into it. He prefers to stay at home and watch TV and tells us that somebody needs to stay on site.

He never likes to leave the site for more than a few hours. He has never minded us going out and tells us that we should go out more often and that he is not an old man that needs looking after.

Ross is great and the three of us are very close. He views Lia as the daughter he never had and she adores him, she sees him as a replacement dad.

Quite often, I have to laughingly drag her back to our chalet after dinner in order that I can have her to myself without her and Ross chattering away about the day's events.

In the winter period we spend more time in Ross's house. That first year, after we had been snowed in for a week, Ross had introduced Lia to Monopoly. Since then, board games are a regular thing we do, especially on a Sunday afternoon.

We are a happy family; I don't know what I would have done without Ross.

I had soon discovered that Lia was a good cook and loved baking. As a result I am now two stone heavier and Lia has gone up two dress sizes. I jokingly tell her she may not fit through the chalet door much longer.

I love her as she is and a few extra pounds would never change that.

I doubt people would recognise us now. I have kept my head shaved, although I may not need to do this much longer as I have noticed that my hair is not growing like it used to.

Lia has grown her hair into a short bob and changed the colour to an ash blonde.

I know that the life we have will not last forever and that one day Ross will no longer be here. He is now in his seventies; he still gets about fine and never complains of being unwell. I just hope he continues in good health and we can at least enjoy another 10 years here.

The absent son has never turned up and as each year went by, Ross mentioned him less and less. He does not mention him now.

I know it pains him that his son has turned his back on his family. I do not mention Aaron to him, it's best not to bring it up.

He has me and Lia, we are his family now and we intend staying for as long as Ross needs us.

We have nowhere to go, we don't want to be anywhere else, this is our life and we couldn't be happier.

To think, we have been here just over 10 years. Lia is 30 today and I intend to make this a great birthday for her along with our friends and guests.

ABOUT THE AUTHOR

Sharon Fellows has lived in various places in the UK and currently resides in the West Midlands.

Printed in Great Britain
by Amazon